Origin Exposed

Descended of Dragons
Book 2

by
Jen Crane

Published by Carpe Noctem Publishing LLC
Edited by Lacey Thacker
Cover Design by Deranged Doctor Designs

Origin Exposed

First electronic publication: October 2015
First print publication: October 2015

Digital ISBN: 978-0-9965756-2-1
Print ISBN: 978-0-9965756-3-8

To Brock
whose love and support of me,
my writing, and our family is more epic
than any fantasy put to paper.

Also by Jen Crane

Rare Form
Descended of Dragons, Book 1

www.JenCraneBooks.com

For news and releases: http://bit.ly/Jen_Crane_Newsletter

Acknowledgments

Where would I be without the kind, patient, and generous author Brinda Berry? Locked away somewhere crying on my keyboard, that's where. Thank you, Brinda, for your innumerable answers to my endless questions. Thank you for reading and improving my books. Thank you for sharing your experience and expertise. Thank you for bracing the wings of fledgling authors like me.

To Lacey Thacker, thanks for an editing process that didn't make me cry. You made it fun; are so supportive, and I appreciate you and your work.

Thanks to author Kathleen Groger for lightning-fast and razor-sharp beta reading.

To fellow authors Megan Mitcham and Lindsay Cross: I can't thank you enough for your immeasurable support through this process. I value our friendship, our writing retreats, and our girl time, though it's too infrequent.

Thanks to my mom, Belinda, for reading and loving these books. Your unconditional support makes me feel invincible, and I sure need that some days.

1

I sat wrapped in Rowan Gresham's strong arms thankful for my life and his.

His warm skin was a welcome contrast to mine as I pressed my cheek to his chest and absently nuzzled his wide shoulder.

But my efforts to relax, to relish the comfort and security Gresham's presence lent were useless. My bare legs trembled to the beat of an erratic heart. What started as a light tremor grew stronger until the physical manifestation of my shock intensified to a full-blown shake. I snapped my knees together and wrapped my arms around them. If the traitorous things insisted on vibrating, I would constrict them into serenity.

My plan didn't work.

I was a ragged mess from the aftermath of the fight with Brandubh, and bewildered to learn not only did I *have* living relatives, I was descended of dragons who were feared, hated.

And my father—about whom I'd sought information my entire life—was a magical breed I'd never heard of: an *omni.* It was urgent I learn more about him, as well as the dragons. It just so happened I had a captive audience of three such dragons.

But as I scoured the mountainous crater in which they'd been imprisoned for centuries, I found no one. My stomach seized at the realization Gresham and I were the only two left on the rocky battlefield. The Drakontos dragons had traced away as we celebrated our victory over the powerful sorcerer Brandubh.

"Gresham."

"Hmm?" He had recovered quickly from the fight, and was nuzzling my neck. His breath was hot on my collarbone and his hand crept dangerously close to my naked ass.

"Gresham," I said. "The dragons are gone."

His dark head snapped up, amber eyes wild as they bounced around the crater. He jerked his hand from me in confused horror. *Like I'd put it there.*

"Dammit," Gresham growled and stood to his full height. "Dammit!" His curse reverberated through the cratered mountain's interior, echoing his frustration. He squeezed his hands into tight fists at his sides, and stopped pacing long enough to stomp a foot. "I can't believe I let them get away." Gresham's every move was rigid with anger. "He'll have my job for this. My job, hell," he spat, "he'll have my head. And rightly so. I had four of Thayer's prime enemies in one place and let them escape. Right under my damn nose."

"Well, that's not really fair, Gresham," I said. "You were knocked unconscious. Brandubh nearly killed us both. He may have gotten away, but just barely. And he must be badly injured if the dragons were able to trace away and escape him."

"He'll heal. They'll heal," he said, kicking a pile of rocks that sent stone and dust flying in a wide arc. "I had them all here and could do nothing. I couldn't use my magic, couldn't trace. It was stupid to come here alone with you. I underestimated him and inflated my own ability. Dammit!"

He stopped pacing and looked me up and down, a scowl replacing his handsome features. A snarl gathered his lips into a bitter pinch. "I continue to make poor decisions where you're concerned, behaving like a teen-aged boy trying to impress a girl."

On some level I preened with pleasure to hear the enigmatic man admit he lost his senses around me, that he wanted to impress me. I'd longed to wow him since the moment I first saw him. But I was also wary of the admission. Rowan

Gresham was sharp, and not just intellectually. I feared if he suspected his feelings for me compromised him he'd have no reservations about cutting me off.

Gresham continued to curse himself, stomping aimlessly within the crater and mumbling as he stabbed his hands through the hair at the sides of his head.

I tried to deflect some of his stress, and to curb the overly-dramatic self-deprecation by pointing out the things we had accomplished. "We may not have captured Brandubh," I said, "but we learned a lot that could help the authorities. Not only is he still very much alive, but his interest in ruling—or destroying—Thayer still exists."

Gresham's eyes compressed to a tight squint. "You're saying that like it's a good thing."

"No…I mean… We learned about his sick dragon-breeding plan. We stopped it. And because we injured him so badly, his remaining dragons were able to escape. He has nothing now."

"Oh, Brandubh will always find a way. Dragons or no, he'll never stop." Gresham stopped his pacing to face me. "I know you're trying to find the positive in the situation, Stella. But let me tell you how the leader of Thayer, the people of Thayer, will see it. I was the first one to see Brandubh in centuries. I stood within feet of him, fought him. Not only did I *not* capture him, but a little girl fought him for me. I allowed him to escape. *And* I failed to discover where he's been hiding all these years."

"I think you're taking this far too personally," I said, but he ignored me. His rant amped even louder, his voice booming throughout the cavernous space.

"I discovered that three of the dragons responsible for the Steward Massacre—until now thought eradicated—are alive. I didn't capture them. No, I allowed them to escape, too, and have no idea where to begin looking for them. Worse, the dragons know I know they exist. They'll assume we're coming for them and go into hiding. Or come for us first."

I crept toward him and reached to console him, but he jerked away before I could touch him. "Why are you acting like it's your sole responsibility to save Thayer?" I asked. "I mean, sure, we're taught at Radix we're supposed to defend our home, but it wasn't your job alone, Gresham. You fought Brandubh; you nearly had him. I injured him, and we cost him his most valuable weapons. Not a bad day."

"Stella," Gresham said, his face crumbling into a tortured mask, "it *is* my job. I've been protecting the people of Thayer since long before you were born."

"But..." I paused, trying to comprehend. "What do you mean? What're you saying?"

Gresham slammed his eyelids shut. He clenched his teeth with such force I saw the muscles working in his square jaw.

"Gresham? You said you did 'special projects.' I knew you were being intentionally vague, but…what…what are you saying?"

He let out a ragged breath and found my gaze. His eyes were pained. Shamed. "There is much I didn't—couldn't—tell you at first. I should've told you when you first found your wolf, but by then I felt such guilt. And I was shocked to find that I *gave a damn*, Stella. I didn't want to see the disappointment in your eyes. I knew you'd find out eventually. I'm surprised it took this long. It only did because you're an outsider and your friends are all primos. I thought for certain the Redfern girl would recognize me from my dealings with her father, or one of those boys you associate with would piece it together."

Blood rushed to my face, my ears. I heard white noise, a faint but consistent background to our conversation.

"What the hell are you talking about, Gresham?" My voice rose as I grabbed at his arm and pulled him around to face me. "Tell me what?" My face was fevered and I felt the familiar sting of tears.

"Stella," he said reverently, smoothing the auburn hair back from my face. He bent to run his dry lips across mine before he said, "My position is director of defense. It's my job to eradicate threats to Thayer."

A burst of air escaped my parted lips and I lay a hand on my heart to make sure it stayed within my chest. I was so shocked

I couldn't take a full breath and sucked short, inadequate gasps of air.

My mind scattered in a dozen directions.

I tried to recall what Gresham had said to me over the course of the weeks I'd known him. I tried to process what I knew of Thayer, of Radix, of alternate forms. Why would someone as important as the Director of Thayerian Defense pursue me? Why would he become my unofficial guardian, injecting himself in my life as a mentor, a friend…a lover? What could he possibly have to gain from his association with someone like me who wasn't of this world, who didn't even know who she was?

The answer hit me like a kick to the chest. I stood heaving, trying to gain control of myself, trying not to completely fall apart. My heart physically hurt at the betrayal, and the tears that had been taunting me finally spilled over and fell hotly onto my cheeks. I bent over and held my middle, a nauseated mass.

Gresham was calling my name, but it seemed so far away. "Stella? Stella, no. No. It's not like that." He spoke almost frantically and rushed to my side.

I jerked from him, but was so off balance I had to extend my hand for support. My knees were weak and there was nothing on which to anchor, so I listed clumsily sideways before catching myself.

I closed my eyes and took several slow breaths before attempting to speak again. Nothing came. I cleared my throat, attempted to clear my mind and aimed for composure, but all I really wanted to do was crumble into a heap in the dirt.

I cursed myself for my naivety, my inexperience, my ignorance. I felt stupid and small.

But after a lengthy interlude of self pity, my mind kicked into gear, and in a moment of clarity—or self-preserving procrastination—it struck me that Rowan Gresham never talked about himself. He certainly never offered details. If he was in a mood to share it would be smarter to save my grief for later, to put my own feelings on hold and hear what he had to say. And so, despite the fact that my heart felt like artisan glass that had splintered with a thousand hairline fractures, I took advantage of the situation. If he was willing to talk, I would listen and endure the pain of his words. I steeled myself for the worst.

"It's not like what, Gresham?" I asked. "That you weren't watching me from the very beginning, that you weren't monitoring my every development?"

His chiseled cheeks filled with air before he blew it out and closed his eyes. It was obvious he'd rather skip this part. "In the beginning, sure," he admitted. "But it was my job to learn more about you; it was my duty to my people. I—"

"Your people?" I interrupted. "*Your* people? Thayer's my home now, too, you know. Are you telling me you found me, brought me here, helped me with school, with my metamorphosis…all to spy on me?"

His brow furrowed in frustration. "Well, when you put it like that it sounds worse than it was, Stella."

"Put it like that?" My voice was loud. Hard. Angry. I had left feeling injured in the dust and was fast approaching enraged. "How else can I put it? It's pretty damn straightforward. And what about the rest? We very nearly slept together. You took advantage of me, knowing the whole time you were using me. You're an assho—"

"Took advantage of you," Gresham scoffed. "You made the first move that night in your room. Do you know the restraint it took to allow you to straddle me for hours and not take you then and there? You'd mounted me already; we were halfway there. I knew you were attracted to me. You'd wanted me for weeks."

"Oh, you couldn't possibly," I sputtered. Gresham was always so bold when he talked about sex. He had used that bravado to intimidate me, to infuriate me, to seduce me. I wasn't sure what his intention was at that moment, but I felt all three.

"I sure as hell could know," he said with a smirk. "And did. Yet I made no move. But you—you woke and rubbed me like a wanton cat. You kissed me like you'd die if you didn't have me, and rode me through our clothes until I thought *I'd* die. Thank god we were interrupted."

Gresham was delusional if he thought he was blameless. I recalled the thoroughness, the possessiveness with which he kissed me in my room. "What about after the attack on Caraway Manor?" I said. "You certainly took charge then."

"After you handed it to me steaming on a platter. The entire room was filled with your desire. No man could walk away from that, Stella. And yet I did, if you'll recall."

I recalled all right. Fragments of Gresham's thoughts had run through my mind the last time we'd been intimate. *Wrong. Stop. Truth.* Soon after he pulled away from me and left with a hoarse "I'm sorry." We hadn't talked about it since.

He shook his head. "I haven't taken advantage of you and you know it."

"What we did physically isn't the point, Gresham. I'm not saying you robbed some virgin of her propriety. I know who and what I want. I'm a big girl with a big girl appetite. I did want you. Hell, I still do, and don't think I don't know how screwed up that is."

"Then what is the point? Get to it, so we can go home and get to what we both want."

I laughed, but it held no humor. "That is so not going to happen because the *point is* you got close to me, befriended me, seduced me. You encouraged me to trust you, to depend on you, and somewhere along the way I started to have feelings for you. And you let me, knowing all the while I had no idea you'd pursued me just to keep an eye on me."

When my eyes fell closed a tired breath escaped my tense mouth. I felt just like the desolate terrain on which I stood. I was the world's biggest fool. And in my insecure imaginings I thought Gresham looked at me every day and saw me as the fool I was for not catching on to his skeevy manipulations.

"I didn't pursue you to seduce you, Stella," Gresham said and grasped my chin so I was forced to look at him. "That was never my plan. Hell, I considered you a child. I had Livia. My intentions were to bring you to Thayer and to monitor your form."

"What if I'd turned into a dragon first, Gresham? What would you have done then?" That's the question I asked, but my knee-jerk jealousy to the mention of Livia was what most occupied my mind. Did he miss her? Was he regretful? Did he consider me immature and inexperienced in comparison?

"If your form had been a dragon, then I would've interceded."

My heart stuttered to a stop at his business-like tone. "What does that mean? Interceded?"

"Thayerian sentiment has been strongly anti-dragon since the Steward Massacre," he said. "You know that. If a new dragon had emerged, an outsider especially, you'd have been assumed savage and condemned before you knew what hit you. The entire situation had the potential for catastrophe. Not just for Thayer, but for you, too."

"You still didn't answer my question. What would you...what *could* you have done if I was a dragon like my mother?"

"I don't know," he said tersely. "But it was important to learn who you were, where your loyalties lie, what your vulnerabilities were."

"Didn't you have some underling that could've done that? Some special agent. If you're so important, couldn't you have sent someone else to spy on me? Surely there are other guys who are more my type if seduction was your goal."

I was hurting. I wanted Gresham to hurt, too. I'd been humiliated, reduced to a mark to be targeted. I thought Gresham was interested in *me*, that I'd grown on him during the time we spent together...like he'd grown on me.

He shook his head, ignoring my jab. "The fewer people who knew about you the better. Livia's premonitions may have alerted me to your existence, but even she didn't piece together you might've been a dragon. I handled you myself to keep those invested to a minimum."

Handled. Ouch. I fought back more tears—I had to remain focused on my endeavor to find more information while Gresham was offering it. "So, the people who know about me are limited to the two of us, the Drakontos dragons, and Brandubh?"

"And Aemon," Gresham said. "He knows."

"Aemon? Professor Lochlain? Why does he know?"

"Well, I had to give him a damn good reason to come with me to your world to get you, for one thing. He's also a trusted friend and an expert on dragon lore."

I scowled at Gresham. "Weren't you afraid he'd pronounce me a primordial savage, too?"

"I wasn't, no. Aemon's as level-headed as they come. And trustworthy."

"So, am I still in danger? Does the fact that I'm half Drakontos mean I'm still heir to enemy status, or does my father's omni heritage negate that?" I didn't know what to think about myself. Maybe Gresham could give me some clue, some direction.

"You know I don't see you as an enemy. Don't be ridiculous. As for you being in danger, that remains to be seen."

His shoulders slumped so low on a tired breath I thought they might touch the rocky ground. "It's complicated. For now, let's leave this pit while we still can. We'll visit Aemon once we've recovered from the shock of the day. You can get to know him. We'll discuss how to proceed, form a plan."

I considered my options. Yes, I wanted to get away from Rowan Gresham as quickly as possible. But where would I go? Back to my room at Sabre Hall? I couldn't tell Timbra; I couldn't tell anyone about my dragon—about all I'd learned. Not yet. With Mom gone, the only people I had left were Gresham and my friends from Radix. My old college roommate, Lizzie, and the rest of the people back home had no clue about this world.

The only ones who knew about my dragon form were people I couldn't trust. That scared the hell out of me. Besides being alone, I was in danger, and I wasn't even sure from whom. The tremors that had died down resurfaced with fury. The trembling wasn't limited to my legs this time, but surged through my body up to my teeth. I snapped my chattering jaws shut, but that only sent the movement through my neck, and my head bobbed like a cork at sea.

"What's wrong?" Gresham searched my face for some indication of the source of my trauma. "What are you thinking?"

My silence had said much. I didn't cry again, but I wanted to. My body hunched over in distress and I cupped my brow trying to squeeze a plan for what to do next from my brain.

I had always thought myself not the type to fold under pressure, that I'd never be pitiful or whine about the unfairness of my circumstances. But dammit, I'd had a real hard day. Infamous but unknown relatives appeared from nowhere only to betray me. Gresham was almiost killed—hell, *I* was almost killed. I tore an evil sorcerer's throat out by my teeth—the first time I ever tried to kill anyone, to my recollection. And the man I fought to save, the one on whom I'd come to trust and depend, admitted he befriended me to spy on me.

I very seriously considered curling my weary body into a tight ball and shutting out the world. I couldn't handle the situation. I wasn't equipped. "I…I can't trust you," I said as my voice cracked with emotion. "I can't talk to anyone about what's going on. I don't have a soul to trust, to confide in. I don't know what to do." My wobbly knees finally gave way and I crumbled to the rock and dust.

"That's just not true, *me cynamome,*" Gresham said and joined me on the ground. "I asked to be in your life, and I meant it. I know what this looks like. I know you doubt my sincerity and feelings for you after what I've done. But you have to believe I was shocked to find you—to find *us*—when my intention was only ever to observe you."

I sniffled. Wiped my nose. "How can you expect me to believe that when you've admitted you deceived me from the start?" I was so tired. So, so tired.

"I don't know," he said and heaved his shoulders. "If we have to start over, if I must work to regain your trust day by day, then it's what I'll do. One advantage to being so long-lived is developing patience enough to eventually acquire what's most valuable to you."

I had no response to that. We sat facing each other in silence on the dusty ground, both at a loss for answers, for direction.

"Gresham?" I finally said.

"Yes?"

"What does 'me sinna moam' mean?"

"Mmm?" he hummed and ran his thumb across my knuckles.

"Me sinna moam. You said that when you argued I could trust you."

"Oh. 'My faire bryd, me swete cynamome.' It's from *The Canterbury Tales*. It reminds me of you. Your cinnamon hair."

"Oh," I said. Real clever response, I know, after a man complimented me with Chaucer.

"I don't know about you," Gresham said and squeezed my hand, "but I'd like to find some pants."

I jerked at the sudden awareness we were having the conversation sans clothes. I hadn't noticed. I was finally becoming accustomed to the forced nudity that came with having more than one physical form. After the initial embarrassment, I smiled.

Hey, you have to celebrate the little victories in the face of such massive failures.

2

Gresham and I traced together to my room at Sabre Hall, and our nudity made the fragile situation that much more awkward.

My subconscious brain chose to ignore my particular reality, and instead rehashed all I had learned over the course of the day. Once the information began trickling in, it forced open a crack that flooded my drowning mind. I had gained a mountain of knowledge about myself, Gresham, the dragons, Brandubh, and of course about my mother and father. I was overwhelmed with information, with emotion. I didn't know what to do next, or how to feel about Gresham…about any of it, really.

Time to decompress was what I really needed. Time to sort everything out, put the different bits of information into their correct mental boxes, and then open them one by one. It was essential that I consider the contents at my own pace and make a plan.

But there was no way that was possible. Even with time, I wouldn't be equipped to handle such pressure. It was all too serious and too depressing and too hard and too damned scary.

A month earlier I'd been a twenty-two-year-old college kid with, okay, no real plans for the future, but also no pressure, no serious concerns. I drank too much and danced a lot. I got my nails done while taking Cosmo quizzes. The biggest challenge I faced was deciding between groceries or a new handbag. I may not have been fulfilled or challenged, but, by god, I was stress-free.

I missed those days. I wanted one of them. I was desperate to be rid of the constant, smothering pressure to study more, learn more, be better. I was sick of regretting the depraved history of my family and tired of worrying about my own potential for depravity.

Ugh, to feel good *for a change.* I was lonely, still in mourning about my mother, and I wanted to forget for just a little while.

"Gresham," I whimpered. He whipped his head up at my tone, sending black hair in disheveled swaths across his forehead. The way I called his name was an entreaty, an appeal.

His wide chest expanded and released on a ragged breath. "I want you; you know this," he said. "But I'll not be accused of taking advantage of you again."

I closed the distance between us and stood just outside of touching, the front of my body so close to his that the heat of him left my back jealous and bereft.

"I know what you've done, Gresham." I held his gaze, forcing him to understand the depth of conviction behind my words. "I know who you are. And right now, I don't care. I want this." My voice cracked as I said, "I *need* this."

Gresham lowered his face with excruciatingly slow deliberation, his gaze never leaving my own even as his lips brushed mine once, twice, back again. When he was satisfied he'd given me every opportunity to change my mind, he took them so softly, so sensually that my addled brain short-circuited. I stood motionless, relishing the pleasure of his breath across my skin, the trace of his fingers along my collarbone, the brush of his thumb over my breast. He lifted my hair and bent to kiss my neck. I arched my spine in response and felt his smile of approval on my skin.

Our kisses grew more frenzied, rougher, but no less sensual as I moved back and forth against him. My breaths left my body in pants.

He pulled his mouth from mine and sought approval in my gaze before ducking to my body again. God, he was so talented. I was so needy, so very turned on.

"I want you now, Stella." Rowan Gresham brooked no argument.

A whispered "Yes," was all I could manage.

He backed me up to the bed, kneading my body and sucking lazily on my lower lip before he released it. His eyes were alight with wicked intentions, and I knew with sudden clarity that I was way out of my depth with him.

I dove in anyway.

I lay back as he stalked over me. That divine scent of earth and spice and man enveloped my senses, and I couldn't deny the ache within me any longer.

Upon catching pieces of his fragmented thoughts earlier, a suspicion started to form. I wondered if we could communicate wordlessly.

"I need you, Gresham."

I didn't have to say it aloud. He'd heard me, all right. His eyes widened and he bit down on his bottom lip, a lazy smile playing at the edges of his mouth.

"Dear gods, Stella, are you trying to make me lose my seed before we've even started?"

"No one calls it 'seed' anymore, Gresham."

"Rowan. When we're together, I want you to call me Rowan."

I tried the name out, rolled it around in my brain, if not yet on my tongue. *"Rowan. I dunno. Seems strange. I've always thought of you as Gresham. I do know that I am* loving *this telepathy."*

"Are you always this chatty in bed?" he asked.

"No, not typically. Guess you bring out the best in me."

"Let's see what else I can bring you to."

He approached me with the confidence, the finesse, of a Spanish bullfighter, and I sucked in a hesitant breath.

"You all right?" he asked and pushed a mass of red hair from my forehead.

I nodded and gave a wicked grin, putting on a front far more confident than I felt.

When he smiled back at me, his amber eyes crinkled at the corners. But the smile was soon lost to another look. This one was darker, possessive, intent.

He found his way smoothly, and if I had any remaining desire to chat, it was replaced by a different desire altogether. I became lost—lost to the exquisite force of his big body, to the feel of his powerful arms surrounding my head, and of his hands in my hair, on my face, on my lips.

He murmured lovers' words next to my ear between kisses. "So good, Stella," and "I never thought we could be like this," or "You're exquisite."

"You always this chatty in bed, Gresham?"

He grinned, gazing down at me as lust battled with amusement.

"Rowan," he said. "I told you to call me Rowan."

Ultimately lust won out. Slow and gentle was replaced by intentional, forceful, as he took my lips and swallowed my uninhibited cries of pleasure.

"I can feel you pulsing around me," he whispered wordlessly through my mind and I groaned with satisfaction. I adored the feel of him inside me as I absorbed his unspoken words, welcoming this invasion into another of my private spaces.

Afterward, Gresham slid beside me and pulled me tightly into him. I instinctively threw a leg over his middle and an arm around his chest. We lay there unspeaking, breathing hard and gathering our thoughts. Making love under the cover of darkness is one thing. Doing it wildly in broad daylight is quite another. There was no concealing darkness to hide anxious expressions, no pretending to sleep to avoid immediate consequences.

Lovers. We were officially lovers. I wondered if he would regret it. Again.

I darted a glance up at him and found him staring at me. An expression I hadn't seen him make before slid across his

face. His lips pulled back into a smug grin; his eyes were languid. So confident, so satisfied. So *male*.
We didn't say anything. There was no need. We simply lay there, enjoying the moment and each other.

3

"Wow. When I pursued you as a suite mate I had no idea you'd be famous," Timbra said, her wide eyes blinking innocently.

"Oh. Shut. Up."

Timbra Redfern was not only my suite mate at Radix Citadel for Supernatural Learning, she was a valued friend. My best friend. That she had adorable furry ears and knobby knees was of no consequence. We all have our little issues. Mine, of course, was that I didn't just turn furry; I also grew scales. Tough, armored scales of auburn and copper covered my body when in one of my new-found animal forms. In my other, I became a massive red wolf.

I only knew one other person who had more than one physical form, and that was my…lover, Rowan Gresham. 'Boyfriend' wasn't a good descriptor. Gresham was decidedly *not* a boy. We hadn't known each other long enough to be partners. Lover would have to do.

Timbra's black eyes eyes were alight with mischief, her long lashes fanning across her cheeks with each blink. "I'm serious! Look around. Every person in this place either wants to *be you* or to *do you*. And I'm definitely going to have to change panties when I get back to my room."

My burst of laughter was accompanied by an involuntary snort.

"Never mind. Not everyone. No way I'm screwing a snorter."

Timbra Redfern was witty and hilarious, but very few people knew it. On the outside she was stunning. Her willowy body looked flawless in any outfit, and she walked with grace. Her presence was always known, and she didn't even try. But on the inside she was quite shy. She preferred blending in. The most striking thing about Timbra, though, was her ears. The velvety pointed things always protruded from the top of her dark honey hair and twitched whenever she was nervous or upset.

Grins were still pasted on our faces as we made our way to the back of On a Roll sushi bar where Boone, Ewan, Layla, and Mari were toasting tiny cups of saki.

Timbra was right; gazes darted and eyes widened as I passed, and my keen hearing picked up fragments of whispers. "That's her!" and "You think it's all true?"

There were a few comments on my appearance that set my spine a little straighter "I'd give a canine for an ass like that," or "That hair; that skin. So exotic."

I caught the end of one "…scrawny whore" and wheeled around, my gut clenching and face reddening as my temper flared at the insult.

Livia. *Dean* Livia Miles, head of Radix's Department of Craft and Ritual. Not my biggest fan. It had been Livia, a talented clairvoyant, who'd alerted Gresham to my existence in the first place. Her visions of me in his bed had been the cause of much contention between the two of them. That Rowan Gresham's bed is exactly where I had ended up lent her psychic abilities real credit. Not that she lacked credibility—she was dean of one of Radix's most important departments, after all. A fact she'd made miserably clear to me at every opportunity.

When I first met her, I thought Livia Miles sophisticated and lovely. Now, heartache and bitterness pinched her features and she looked thinner, older. I did feel some regret for the way things had ended between she and Gresham. On the night of their breakup she found me in Gresham's home dressed in nothing but his white button-down shirt. The circumstances had been innocent enough, but Gresham let her believe we'd been intimate. I thought this a fairly callous move on his part, but Livia Miles was nothing if not calloused already. She could handle it.

In fact, it looked as if she was on a date. With none other than the sandy-haired Sabre Bar playboy and bartender Knox Mahon. Livia made a big show of rubbing her fingers playfully over his and then focusing her undivided attention on his every brogue and burr. *Message received, Livia,* I thought. *You've moved on. I'll be sure to tell Gresham. Like* hell.

"Ah, here comes Dragon Lady now," quipped Boone as we neared the table. "Take my seat, ma'am. Please."

"Oh, you guys are freakin' hilarious, aren't you?" All of the attention, good-natured ribbing or not, made me uncomfortable. I didn't like having a spotlight shone on me. I much preferred to blend into the background—especially among these people, whom I'd come to love and trust.

"I told her that everyone here wants to do her or be her," said Timbra. "She thinks I'm exaggerating."

Enthusiastic 'mm-hmm's' and 'I know dat's right's' erupted, but one face remained stony. Ewan. He turned his dark head from me and mumbled something almost inaudibly. He'd been in such a bad mood lately.

"What's that?" I asked.

Ewan Bristol's shiny black curls fell in layers almost to the top of his shoulders in back, and just around his temples in the front. No hair was in its proper place, but it was perfect just the same. Big, dark-brown eyes with nearly-curly black lashes topped the slender slope of his nose, which skimmed over slight nostrils and into cheeks that looked downy smooth when contrasted to the perpetual five o'clock shadow that ran the length of his jawbone. A hint of a mustache brought attention to his lips, which thrust out in an almost child-like pout.

"I said, 'My nose never lies. Someone's already doing her.'" He finally raised his chestnut eyes to mine and his rugged jaw thrust forward with determination. He stared me down, his expression revealing such disgust that I jerked, horrified.

The restaurant went silent. It wasn't just quiet, but as if all of the sound in the room had been sucked out by a solar system-sized gravitational pull—a black hole, an absence of sound. My ears roared as humiliation pumped blood to them, and my cheeks flushed so quickly they stung. Words escaped me and my mouth fell open in surprise. Ewan had always been so reserved, so polite.

I darted glances to Timbra, to Layla, to Boone. They all showed varying degrees of shock. Boone's sharp jaws sat agape, Timbra's fingertips hastily shot up to cover her mouth, and Layla's lips formed a perfect "o." Ewan's comments were so out of character he'd stunned the entire table.

As the blood slowly drained from my face and my shamed haze cleared, I found the other patrons weren't hanging on our every word, but were eating, having their own conversations. My humiliation was mitigated to our table, at least. I avoided any further eye contact with my friends and fiddled nervously with a napkin. Several deep breaths did nothing to help me calm down, to move on, so I excused myself and raced toward the bathroom.

I'd gotten nearly twenty feet when I heard a strained voice call, "Stella, wait."

Ewan, who'd followed me, grabbed for my elbow, but I shook him off and increased my pace.

"Stella. Please. I'm sorry I said that."

I slowed and turned, letting him see the hurt, the questions in my eyes.

"Well, how the hell did you expect me to feel?" He shook his head, his handsome face pinched into something bewildered and angry.

"What are you talking about," I hissed.

"The last we saw each other, I—I thought we had something real." His infinite gaze searched mine. "Hell, *you* pursued *me*. You kissed me. You felt as strongly as I did the connection between us. I know you did. Then, out of nowhere,

I smell Gresham all over you. And Boone confirmed you've been seeing him."

"Oh, what does Boone know?" I scoffed. "He knows nothing."

"He knows what Timbra knows." That hurt. I hadn't expected she would share the details of my love life. "Surely you're not denying it?"

"No, I'm not denying it, Ewan." I circled a thumb along my temple to ease some tension. "We…we got to know each other during my metamorphosis training. We've been through a lot together. It just happened. I don't know."

"And you'll continue to see him?"

"Yes," I admitted, and he flinched ever so slightly.

"Didn't you think you owed me some kind of explanation?" he asked, his voice growing lower in pitch with each word until it was almost a growl. "Did what was between us ever cross your mind?"

I huffed out a breath. "Of course I thought about it. I did. But I heard you were seeing Pippa and I chalked our make-out sessions up to…I don't know…drunken flirting."

He didn't just flinch that time. He balked. Ewan had deeper feelings for me than I'd realized, that much was obvious.

My insides turned over in shame and I snapped my eyes shut, unable to meet his gaze again after comprehending how thoughtless I'd been. The restaurant's small dining room expanded and stretched until I was forced upon a tiny dais for all the world to inspect. I felt minuscule. More than just an insensitive love interest, I had been a bad friend. A bad person. While it was no defensible excuse, my treatment of Ewan was probably the result of being so used to the hook-up culture of my college town before coming to Thayer. He didn't deserve that, and he obviously hadn't expected it of me.

I finally looked up to find Ewan's face strained. His deep eyes held anger, rejection, pain…and restraint. A lot of restraint.

"I'm sorry for what I said," he offered again. "It was crude." Then he stood to his full height, using the significant advantage to drive home his next point. "For what it's worth, I thought we had the potential for something legendary." He leaned in close to me, his breath a puff on my forehead beneath my scattered hair. "And Stella?" he said, barely above a whisper as he ran a finger from the top of my shoulder down my bare arm.

"Yes?" I managed before a compulsory swallow.

"I still do."

With that mic-dropper, he turned his back to me and stalked toward our friends.

In the restroom, I attempted to compose myself, trying and failing not to feel like a real asshole. My mirrored reflection revealed too much. It seemed to amplify my flaws, which had stacked so high I might never reach the top in order to clear them. But improving myself was necessary, no doubt about it. I had mistreated Ewan. Badly. I couldn't feel sorry about Gresham, but did regret my gross insensitivity.

I liked Ewan, who'd proved to be an exceptional person. It might take a while but I hoped I could regain his trust. Eventually, maybe he could even forgive me.

Resolved to be a better person, my true image was reflected in the mirror once more. Someone once told me I looked like a Scot and an Italian had been thrown into a blender. My auburn hair was long and a little wild. But rather than pale or freckled skin, mine was olive. My face was filling out my big features as I grew older. I'd been a gangly kid with a big mouth and over-large eyes. Cute, but never pretty.

After reapplying lip gloss, I made my way back to our table. It took a lot of effort; quite a bit of humility, but I smiled at my friends to show that all was well…or that it would be.

Relief flooded me when the waiter arrived to take our orders and broke the tense atmosphere. "Ah, Ms. Stonewall," he said and pushed his smeared glasses higher up on his nose. "It's a pleasure to have you. Whatever you like, it's on the house."

"No! Thank you for the gesture. But no. I enjoy your food and I'm happy to pay."

"I insist. My mother's people were Fae. My parents told me the tale of the Steward Massacre, just as I tell my children and they will tell their own. Each generation must know that we lost many in those days. Mothers cleaved to babes in cellars while caves were set afire by those demon dragons. We lost much." A lock of gray hair fell over one eye and he brushed it aside with his pen. "Too much." His milky eyes came back into focus and found mine. "Whatever you like. It's on the house. Anyone who takes on Brandubh is honored here," he said with finality.

I felt humbled. And beyond saddened to hear of his loss. It was clear that arguing further would only be taken as ungracious, and lord knew a lack of grace was one of my flaws.

"I'm sorry for your loss," I said with appropriate gravity. "And thank you for your generosity. I would love a Shiso Crazy roll and some edamame to start, please."

It was several strained moments before the group moved past the awkward tension between Ewan and I, and the horrific tale of the waiter's ancestors. But Boone, bless him, took up the charge.

"Ah, I hate to kill the vibe we've got going here," he said, his voice laced with sarcasm, "but Timbra and I have some news."

Heads swung in his direction. Everything about Boone Adder was big. He was very tall, his rounded eyes and slim nose over-large. His big mouth housed strong white teeth. But it all worked together to form a gentle puppy-face—likely no coincidence since his animal form was a dog. His forbearers evolved from ancient Greek Molossions, massive sandy-colored guards charged with protecting flocks and families.

"We're together," Boone informed the group.

The same heads swung again but toward each other with brows wrinkled in confusion, each reaction echoing the same thought.

Mari was the one who spoke up. "I thought that was common knowledge. I mean, we've all watched you flirt for weeks, but lately you've been, well, schmoopy. You can't stop touching. She looks at you like she depends on you for breath. I've caught you grinning like a fool twice already tonight." She shrugged good-naturedly. "Of course you're together."

"What she said," concurred Layla, whose pixie-short hair was currently died a lovely shade of pink that complimented her brown skin. She wore a thin tank top, no bra, and distressed jeans with barely-there heels. Layla always made a statement. Tonight her ensemble said, 'The only thing sweet about me is the hair.' The white tank was low enough that the black and aqua tattoo spanning her chest was on full display. A two-headed raven began at her collarbone and extended down into her slight cleavage. The ravens' heads stretched, open-mouthed, toward her shoulders as if cawing before taking flight upon a pair of outstretched wings.

"I guess—I guess we just wanted to make it official." Boone would not be deterred from his grand announcement.

"What's official?" Bex had decided to join us. The stunning lioness knew how to make an entrance; I'd give her that. She threw her long caramel hair behind her as she took a chair with great ceremony.

"Boone and Timbra are together," said Ewan.

"That's news?" Bex feigned a yawn before sliding her feline eyes in my direction. "Stella, is it true you tore out Brandubh's throat? Your form's a wolf, then?"

And there it was.

I knew everyone had questions. Hell, I still had a lot of questions. Yes, I was going to have to talk about the night of the Brandubh attack eventually, but I had been avoiding it. Most people, even my close friends like Timbra, knew only the highlights. Gresham and I were led into a trap where we were attacked by Brandubh. Three dragons were present. I severely injured Brandubh by turning into my wolf. Brandubh and the three dragons escaped, though not together. The dragons were no longer under Brandubh's command.

That I had a form besides my wolf was *not* common knowledge.

If only I could escape the inevitable and avoid the entire conversation. But I knew the best course of action, since asked directly in a room full of people, was to be forthcoming. No sense hiding, especially considering how unfair human nature can be. In the absence of the truth, people are more than happy to speculate. Problem was, I wasn't prepared to admit the whole truth. Not yet. Not in a restaurant full of people. Not even to my closest friends.

I would have to evade Bex's question. As luck would have it, I'd had some recent experience with tactical evasion. Gresham was a master, but I was learning to read him and catch his subtle hedging. And learning how to employ the maneuver myself.

"I turned into a wolf, yes." There. That was true.

"And were there really dragons there?" she asked.

"Yes."

Her golden eyes were wide with excitement. She leaned toward me, her shoulders bunched. "What was that like? Were they demented? Did they try to scorch you? I heard you ripped Brandubh's throat out, but how did you escape the dragons?" Bex was the one asking the questions, but the entire table hung on our every word. The tables around us probably listened in, too. Senses in Thayer were heightened, hearing definitely included. *Careful, Stella*, I thought. The details of that day had been kept close to my chest for a reason.

It was necessary to keep the secret, but I felt compelled to defend the Drakontos dragons. While on the surface their actions were indefensible, what wasn't common knowledge was that Brandubh forced them to do those horrific things. He literally controlled them with metal torques, stealing their free will and bidding them to hunt and kill. I knew from my long experience with my mother that the kindest, most innocent soul could be forged into an indiscriminate weapon. But I wasn't certain that people like my friends, who'd feared and hated dragons their entire lives, could ever see them in another, more blameless light.

Still I had to try.

"Actually, the dragons were prisoners there. They didn't want to hurt me." *Well, maybe Stryde did.* "When I defeated Brandubh their torques…shorted out…and the dragons traced away, leaving the metal bands behind. I don't know where they went, but it wasn't with Brandubh. They were eager to escape him. For centuries they suffered and were tortured in their cratered prison, forced to stay in their dragon forms so long that they grew madder with each passing day."

I glanced up to gauge their reactions to my statement. Nearly every head in the group had turned so that an ear faced me—as if they hadn't quite heard right. Ewan's brow held deep grooves of confusion and Boone cleared his throat conspicuously.

"One more reason to eradicate their scaly asses," Bex jeered, her full lips pulled back in disgust.

Her comment received far more support than I liked from our table. Yes, Gresham and I had been right to withhold my relation to the dragons. Fair or not, they were the face of the Massacre.

4

Stella Stonewall
Student Journal Entry #7
Logged via Pia
Saturday, June 28

Some days seem to evaporate in a matter of minutes while others drag on interminably.

Before coming to Thayer and enrolling at The Root my life was damned tedious. Days ran into each other; none bearing any real distinction from the one before it. There was no purpose or substance. Oh, sure, one day I might take a physics test and paint my toenails purple. The next I would study for biology and opt for a margarita instead of Mich Ultra. But in life's grand design mine had no real meaning. My reality sucked.

Then Rowan Gresham introduced me to another world, the one of my parents, and my reality changed. Not only did I discover that my life had purpose, I discovered what I knew of myself was woefully insufficient. I wasn't just a regular girl with regular problems. I was born of a dragon mother and a omni father—a rare species capable of changing into any animal form.

Here in Thayer people are derived of many species, not just apes. Some of my best friends turn furry on the regular. Having an alternate form is normal. Not so normal? Having two alternate forms…or more. So far, when faced with immediate physical danger, I've changed into both a massive red wolf and a fearsome dragon with scales of auburn.

My mother recently abandoned me rather than reveal information about her past. This affects my present. A lot. The pain of her betrayal haunts me every day, but I'm learning how to navigate life with an emotional handicap. And it's a good thing, too, because I just suffered another sickening treachery.

I have three living relatives: a grandma, an uncle, and a male cousin. They're my mother's people, the Drakontos, and are believed to be the last of the dragons.

Though at first I was thrilled to find living relatives, the Drakontos and I will not be playing horseshoes at the family picnic anytime soon. They betrayed me to Brandubh, who had imprisoned them for hundreds of years. He forced them to carry out savage attacks throughout Thayer. It was violent retaliation for one of these attacks, the Steward Massacre, that led to the near-eradication of all dragon lines.

And they set me up to be captured by this guy! They claimed not to know the familial connection until it was too late. I know they'd been tortured for centuries, but how could they want for anyone what they'd suffered, relative or not?

Both Gresham and I nearly died when Brandubh tried to enslave me, too. The sicko had planned an incestuous breeding program in order to repopulate the dragon lines. I was to be a brood mare, or vibria, as fertile female dragons are apparently called. Blech. Still gives me the heebie-jeebies to think about it.

A vision may have alerted Brandubh to my existence, but it didn't reveal all of my secrets. He didn't know that my father was an omni, and he sure as hell didn't know that I had inherited the trait. When he least expected it I changed to wolf form and nearly ripped his throat out. He narrowly escaped. Now I fear his return every day, though Gresham says that we have taken the precautions necessary to thwart a future attack. My surroundings, and even my body are heavily warded against him with powerful magic.

And if all else fails, I am still a badass wolf/ dragon girl that can fight like a boss.

5

"Stella, a physical communication has been accepted for you at Sabre Hall's front desk."

I knew that voice.

"Pia, is it so hard for you to say 'letter?' I know you have a thesaurus function somewhere in that big brain of yours."

"Stella, a letter has been accepted for you at Sabre Hall's front desk."

"There. Isn't that better to you?" I asked.

"No. To me, 'physical communication' has a certain *je ne sais quoi*. But I am programmed to discover the method that will best assist you. If you require a less complex language format, I will simplify for you in the future."

I grunted at her insult. "Speaking of a thesaurus, Pia, you got any synonyms for 'smartass computers?'"

"Will 'insolent intelligence' do, or shall I keep searching, Stella?"

"No, that'll do, Pia. That'll do."

The letter was short and cryptic, but I understood the message. More importantly, I knew who had sent it. Bay, my…grandmother. The one I'd recently discovered. The one responsible for god knew how many horrific deaths during the Steward Massacre. Also, the one who'd attacked me and betrayed me to Brandubh.

To say I had low expectations for the meeting was the understatement of the century.

Gresham didn't know where I was going. I didn't tell anyone. Was that stupid? Probably. I never claimed to be the sharpest knife in the drawer. That old adage 'Fool me once, shame on you. Fool me twice, shame on me' replayed over and over in my mind like a foreboding soundtrack to my certain demise.

But folded into Bay's letter had been a picture of my mother as a girl. The photo wasn't labeled, but I knew right away who the splotchy redhead was. Radiant green eyes stared out at me. They were eager eyes, innocent. I'd never known my mother when her eyes expressed anything besides regret. Bay had obviously meant the photo as an olive branch. She probably knew I couldn't refuse an offering of information on my mom. And so I was going to meet her.

Radix was so heavily warded that the campus wasn't an option for the meeting. I traced just outside of the designated meeting point, which was within hearing distance of The Root, but still outside its warded boundaries.

I didn't see Bay right away and walked toward the rough-hewn stone bridge and sat on a deteriorating wooden bench to wait.

Watching the Basel River flow by proved too peaceful an endeavor for my mood, so I stood. Sat back down. Stood again, and then began to pace. The sting of a cuticle bit to the quick snapped me back into the present. She was late. *Is she coming? Is this another trap?* I didn't think so, but I'd already proven myself naive where my family was concerned. *I should leave.* No amount of information was worth being set up again.

I turned toward the bridge, back toward The Root, and that's when I saw her.

Bay Drakontos' dull-gray hair only held an occasional auburn streak. She wore it down. It was curly, like mine. Like my mother's. But I wouldn't have known her if it weren't for those eyes. They were the same dead green, like trodden moss, that revealed such shame when I discovered she'd betrayed me. I could never forget those eyes.

At the moment they held sorrow and…hope. I nodded acknowledgment, uncertain what to say. She had requested the meeting. I intended to let her start.

"Stella, dear," she began. If she saw my jolt and ensuing smirk at the endearment she ignored it. "I know no apology can ever be enough for the wrongs I've done you. But I want you to know I'm sorry. I can never make you understand the hold he had on us, and I will'na even try. I'll just say…I wish I'd allowed him to kill me before setting that trap for you. Now I know you're one of us, that you're my Edina's, I would rather ha' died than allow him to own you, too."

She left the words there on the riverbank. Left them to sink into the viscous mud of my mind. Neither of us said a word. I swallowed hard and turned to face the river as I thought about my mother, about the fear that gripped her so acutely she couldn't be reasoned with to help me in such a desperate time. And then I thought, maybe there was a way I could get the answers I needed after all.

Can I forgive Bay? I wondered. If I truly believed the dragons weren't culpable in the Steward Massacre, that they were only weapons that Brandubh had used, then I had to. *Didn't I?* But there are varying degrees of forgiveness, and forgiving doesn't have to mean forgetting.

I settled for cordiality and the pursuit of information about my mother.

I intended to be cordial. I did. But my mouth had another idea. "You knew who I was," I accused. "You said you recognized me at the attack on Gresham's house, and still you helped Brandubh trap me. If he'd been successful I'd be with you in that crater right now."

"We didn't send the letter, dear—"

"Don't you dare call me 'dear' again," I seethed.

"All right," she nodded. She closed her eyes and took a deep breath. "Brandubh sent the letter. He lured you to the crater. We were just there, once again pieces to be maneuvered in his endless games."

"But you called us into the crater, out into the open from our cover in the passageway. You could have warned us. We could have gotten away if you'd told us what Brandubh planned."

"You were stuck inside with us the moment you entered the crater, Stella. He planned it all so tediously. Once you arrived you couldn't trace home. You know that. I saw you try. You were stuck like the rest of us."

"We could have run back through the tunnel and outside. Traced from there. You could've warned me, Bay." My voice had risen in pitch, in tension, in volume. I neared screeching at her and forced an inhale so as not to lose it completely.

"There was no way out." She shook her head sadly. "We've been under his control for centuries, dea—Stella. When Brandubh sets a trap, it's exhaustive. He's powerful and thorough."

"Yeah, and you're a traitorous bitch." I hadn't thought the thought before it flew from my mouth. I had a lot of pent-up resentment. Obviously.

"You're right, of course," Bay mumbled. The set of her shoulders and her overall downtrodden demeanor was so much like my mother's at that moment my heart lurched in my chest. Bay had been beaten down. Belittled and tortured just like my mother. Another strong, powerful woman reduced to a cowering shell.

I hated Brandubh. I wanted to kill that motherfucker; to break him like he'd broken my family. At the thought of tearing his throat out a redolent memory saturated my senses. I smelled the rusty vitality, tasted the tinny lava of his life force. I wished like hell I'd taken more. I wished I'd taken it all.

We were both silent for a time. Me, as I tried to check my vengeful rage and Bay, as she no doubt battled her own inner demons.

"Where is Eiven?" I asked. "And Stryde. Are you in hiding? Where did you go that day?"

She nodded, glad to change the subject. "We've a place to hide for now. It's not much, but we're happy to have it. To be free. We're grateful to you for that, Stella. We can never repay you for helping us finally escape Brandubh."

My shoulders shrugged under the weight she put behind her words.

I did wonder, though, not just for them but for myself. "Are you afraid he'll find you? Do you think he can?"

"Aye, I don't think we'll ever stop fearing that."

"What will you do?" I asked. *What should I do*, I wondered.

"We're working on wards to camouflage ourselves. Brandubh shielded us for so long we have a good idea how he did it. We still have some old friends left, some powerful friends. We're close to finding a way."

"Oh, good," I said. "Good." I ran a narrow leaf from a nearby bush through my fingers.

"Eiven and Stryde would like to see you again," Bay said and darted a nervous glance at me. "We'd like to hear about your life, about you, your mother."

My mother. Every time I thought about her my teeth snapped together. I breathed hard through my nose, trying to rid myself of the disgust and disappointment and loss I felt at the mention of her. I looked down to discover I'd ripped the leaf in my fingers to shreds.

"I need to get back," I said. "I…I'm glad you contacted me."

She smiled then—a real smile that reached her dull eyes. She released a breath I imagine she'd been holding for the length of our meeting.

"Would you come for dinner tomorrow?" She darted another glance at me. "To see Eiven and Stryde. To get to know each other. I never dreamed I had a granddaughter. I'd love to know you, Stella."

There is very little else she could have said to affect me more. I'd never had a family. Only my mother. I had desperately wanted a father, a granny, an aunt, cousins. Family, like all of the other kids I knew. The little girl inside me jumped and clapped "Yay!" at the idea.

"Yes," I dared whisper. "Yes."

6

Gresham was waiting in my room when I returned from meeting Bay.

She'd given me instructions to find their new home for the impending dinner. She didn't ask me not to tell Gresham, but I didn't mention seeing her, or my plans for the following night. I knew he wanted to capture them. He'd said as much in the crater after they disappeared. Did that mean he wanted to interrogate them? Prosecute them? Worse? I was afraid to ask, and not entirely sure he'd tell me the truth anyway. Things were strange and volatile and I wasn't certain how I felt about it all. Until I was, I resolved to keep my relationship with the Drakontos dragons close to my chest.

Gresham leaned against my buffet table looking as confident and in control as ever. He smiled when he saw me. That smile. It started off slow and sexy, one side of his lips pulling up into a lascivious smirk. I was a sparrow in the predatory sights of a hawk. He swooped toward me and I couldn't breathe. Rowan Gresham excited and weakened me all at once.

"I've been thinking about our last time together," he said.

"Have you?" I had, too...despite the myriad other things I had to think about.

"Mmm. I can think of little else." He ran a finger along my collarbone, and chills tickled down my spine.

"It's been days since I've seen you," I breathed. "Thought maybe you'd forgotten."

"Forgotten? No chance of that." His eyes held such heat, such single-minded intent, that I shivered at their implication. "But I could stand a reminder."

He backed me up, pushed me against the wall, and pulled my hands over my head. He held my hands in place with one of his and bent to kiss me. My breath hitched as the heat of his mouth competed with the cool brushes of his hair on my skin. In that competition, I was the lucky winner.

He pulled away from me long enough to say, "Hold on," before clasping me to him and tracing from my room at Sabre Hall.

A flash of light, a surge of cold air, and we were at Gresham's home, Caraway Manor. There wasn't time to be disoriented. Gresham consumed me and kissed me urgently the moment we landed in what I assumed was his bedroom. A gigantic plush bed occupied the space between two floor-to-ceiling windows, and a sitting area was just off the bedroom. It was all very vintage masculine chic—clean lines, rich colors, mahogany accents. The furniture flanked a large fireplace, its mantel supporting an oil painting of Caraway Manor and grounds.

"Something wrong with my place?" I panted. We stood at the end of his luxuriously masculine platform bed once he finally released me.

"I thought I might need room to maneuver."

I moaned my approval.

Gresham grabbed the hem of my shirt and pulled it over my head before tossing it aside without another look. He removed his own shirt and wrapped his arms under mine, clasping me to him. He was on fire, his light body hair a sweet abrasion to my charged skin as he moved to kiss my neck and shoulders. I shivered at the feel of his fingers beneath the waistband of my jeans. I took a deep breath, luxuriating in the affectionate foreplay and anticipating his next move.

Gresham guided me back until the backs of my knees met the end of the bed and lay me down. He removed my jeans with precision and then slowly ran his hands up my thighs. "*I love to look at you,*" he whispered across my mind. He drew back to hold my gaze before devouring every inch of my body. I writhed under his attention, ran my fingers through his thick hair, traced the smooth curves of his ears.

Rowan Gresham made me feel alive, eager, elated…like a woman who knew what she needed from a man, and never failed to get it.

I was still breathless when he climbed between my knees and lifted me by the hips up onto his thighs. He wasn't as gentle the second time as he was the first and I dimly thought, *Aha. This is what they mean when they say 'until you can't walk the next day.'*

That was the last time I thought coherently. Rowan Gresham had everything under control. I threw my hands above my head, scratching for purchase of the pillow, the top of the mattress, anything.

I held on for life and let go.

Before coming to Thayer, before meeting Rowan Gresham, I'd been with a couple of boys. They were invariably the same: clumsy and over-anxious novices who saw seduction as embarrassing, as a weakness. So many boys I'd known thought girls were nothing but holes to poke their sticks in. Those who'd taken the time and effort to learn how to please a woman, in my limited view, were few and far between. Why didn't boys realize that having a rep as *en fuego* in the sack would get them laid so much more often?

Sex with Rowan Gresham was so different from my past experiences it deserved another name.

"Do you have plans tomorrow night?" Gresham asked as he thrummed his fingers idly on my thigh.

We lay on our backs, recovering, but at his question I turned to face him.

"I do, actually. Why?"

"I want to take you to Aemon. Since he's known about you from the beginning, and knows a lot about your family's history, he wants to get to know you. He can also help us with a strategy forward."

"Oh." I chewed the inside of my jaw so I didn't give too much away.

"What are you doing?" A line formed between Gresham's brows in suspicion.

"Hmm?"

"What are your plans that you can't meet Aemon tomorrow?"

"Oh. Um, study group," I lied.

Why did I lie? And what did it say about me that I lay in post-coital bliss with a man I obviously didn't trust? Yeah, I so didn't want to go there. I wasn't ready to tell him about my impending meeting with Bay, Eiven, and Stryde. I was allowed to have secrets. Anyway, Gresham had more secrets than I liked to let myself admit.

"Tuesday, then?" he suggested, though he still eyed me suspiciously.

"Sure. Great," I said. Anyone who missed my lack of enthusiasm was simply choosing to ignore it.

7

The hell am I doing here? I asked myself for the tenth time. I must have turned around half a dozen times along the way. To my grandma's house.

But I knew what I was doing. I couldn't fool myself, hard as I tried. The scenario played in my mind over and over. Yes, my newfound grandmother, uncle, and cousin had been accomplices in a trap set for me. But they'd been tortured for centuries; they'd even endured de-winging for not being forthcoming about my existence. And Bay had been so sincere about starting fresh and getting to know me, *her granddaughter*. I wanted family desperately. Even more so after the acute loss of my mother.

"Stella. How lovely to see you," Bay said as I approached the dilapidated wood structure. It was so submerged within the trees, so overtaken by dense branches and leaves, that it looked in danger of an immediate takeover on all sides by the forest itself.

Bay sat atop a stool roughly hewn from a log whose cohorts likely fueled the nearby fire. She leaned toward the fire, her knobby fingers turning some sort of large fowl on a pole suspended above the flames.

"We're still getting used to cooking our food," she said when she noticed my attention on the spit. "There's an old wood oven inside, but it heats the house up."

"Smells delicious," I said and found my own cut log. "What is it?"

"Turkey. Wild turkey. I made some cornbread, too," she said, nodding her head at a cast iron skillet placed just outside the flames.

"It's peaceful out here. This your place?"

"No," she said, her attention still primarily on the food. "An old friend's. Anything we had is gone by now. But this cabin'll do. It's safe."

I nodded. "Not many know you're back, then?"

"No. Just a few people we used to know. That we trust."

"What will you do?" I swallowed past the lump in my throat and cleared my throat. "If someone finds out you're here…that you're alive…" I couldn't finish the thought. We both knew how volatile the situation was.

"Aye, we'll have to hide for now. There are still many who would recognize us."

"But you can't stay here forever. Can't stay concealed forever. Right? Hiding in the woods after such a long imprisonment can't be easy. Surely you miss your old lives."

She lay the pole on its brace and faced me. Her expression was bleak, but not hopeless. A little light still shone in her eyes. Dim, but it was there. "We can do anything when faced with such an alternative," she said. "And we aren't unhappy here, dear—er, Stella. We're free, we can remain in our primary forms now. There's plenty of game to hunt." The force of her smile stacked one wrinkle on top of another as she said, "I've even begun a garden."

"She nearly broke our backs clearing a spot for it, but she's got a garden," Eiven said good naturedly. He emerged from the cabin carrying three glasses of a cloudy brown liquid. "Care for a beer?" he asked while shoving one in my direction. It was lukewarm and smelled so strongly of hops and yeast my cheeks puckered before I'd even had a drink. I took a small sip at first, and while it was strong, it was undeniably delicious.

"My old recipe. But I didn't make this batch." Eiven's red hair demanded attention. It was coarse and thick and stood straight up from his head like a thousand hot needles. A slightly bulbous nose hung over thin lips and lay a shadow over his narrow chin. The wrinkles at the corners of his eyes were better described as tracks, for they were physical indicators of the hard road he'd traveled. But despite his difficult history, his eyes still held kindness.

"It's good that you have friends to help you," I said. "Is there anything I can do?" I blame my dang Southern compulsions again. That offer was far more generous than I felt.

"No, but thank you," he said with a tight, gracious smile. "We've more than we need."

Once I noticed the nervous energy, it became apparent in their every movement. Both Bay and Eiven were tightly restraining themselves. It was more than being on their best behavior. They were both rigid with nerves, the simplest actions seeming to take a mountain of restraint. I swallowed to wet my dry mouth. *Are they hiding something? Are they volatile?* I jerked at the thought. *Are they preparing to attack me? Where's Stryde?*

Instinctively, I thought to trace from danger—score one for this new Thayerian—but then I noticed Bay's hand shaking as she worked to pull the turkey from the spit. It took her every concentration to maneuver the bird to a nearby platter.

Understanding struck. They were still fighting to control their human forms. They'd been dragons so long that manipulating arms and fingers were no longer first nature to them.

I took a shaky breath and helped Bay with the food.

"Where's Stryde?" I asked once we entered the cabin and he wasn't inside.

Bay and Eiven shared an inscrutable look before she replied, "Burning off some extra energy, dear. He'll be along shortly."

I let the 'dear' pass, cognizant of other, more tangible concerns.

The cabin was stale. Somewhat dark, naturally, with no electricity and only a few windows thrown open to facilitate an earthen breeze. Apart from the cleared garden, the trees were so large and thick that sunlight barely made its way down to the forest floor, where layers of old leaves formed sodden paths.

Eiven and I were seated at the farm-style kitchen table. He slammed another home-brew and I took an extra-large swig of my own. It seemed we all needed a crutch to calm our nerves.

Bay wasn't exactly homemaker material, I was pleased to note, as muffled curses floated from the kitchen. Bay was hard, capable, calloused. At home in the kitchen, but in a utilitarian way.

"Did you teach my mother to cook?" I asked before I even considered the question.

She started at my unexpected question but turned toward me, her eyes glassy with unshed tears. She nodded nostalgically. "I did at first. But she was more comfortable in the kitchen than I ever was. Her talents surpassed mine while she was still young."

"I can attest to her skills," I said with a smile. "I loved her cooking. I would choose her pot roast or homemade mac and cheese over going out most times. Which was fine with her. She was something of a homebody."

Bay and Eiven smiled at my fond memory, but their looks soon turned regretful.

"I'm sure she did the best she could," Bay said. "It's hard to be around people again…after."

We fell silent, the mood having taken a dramatic turn for the depressing.

"Who's hungry?" Eiven forced out.

"Shouldn't we wait for Stryde?" I asked. "Or was he really not keen on getting to know me better? You don't have to be nice for him. This situation is difficult for all of us."

"No, he wanted to be here," said Eiven as he passed me the platter of turkey. "It's just…things were harder for him. He's having difficulty adjusting. Bay and I led full lives before our imprisonment. Stryde, he was so young when we were taken. And things were so hard for so long. Somewhere along the way he forgot there was more to life than manipulation and pain. More than bitterness and revenge. It's hard for him to imagine a new life for himself."

"Oh," I breathed. "I'm sorry."

"He's getting better," Eiven assured me. "Every day we try to help him find something positive. Something to look forward to. But he's still fighting a tougher battle than we are."

"When it's just us, he's free to be himself; it's all right if he falters," Bay added. "But with you here, I think he fears he'll fall apart."

"I see." And I did. The extent of my hardships had been a little emotional instability—a mother on the far side of wacky, daddy issues, and, okay, recent uncertainty about my otherworldly parentage and magical abilities. Not to mention my mother's abandonment. But by then I was a grown woman. I hadn't faced centuries of physical torture and manipulation that had nearly driven me to madness. I was still quite sane. *Fairly* sane, at any rate.

"Tell us about your childhood," Bay asked. "If it's not too sad?"

"No, it's all right. My mother…she was nurturing and sweet. She made my Halloween costumes by hand, helped me with my homework. Encouraged my independence by making me feel safe and loved. The only home I ever knew was a small town in the southern U.S. I had a lot of friends...a typical childhood, despite being maybe overly focused on church and religion. I guess she found religion after the tragedies she lived through. It's probably what helped her survive them. She committed her life to God, to her church. She walked the walk. Or maybe tightrope is a better term," I added with a sad grin.

"It sounds lovely, dear," Bay said. "I wish I could have seen you grow up. I'm sorry that I didn't."

"It *was* lovely," I ducked my head, staring into my lap until the threat of tears passed.

I cleared my throat and looked up to find Stryde's bulky body occupying the doorway.

"Hello, Stryde," I croaked.

"Stella," he said, nodding formally and taking a seat at the table.

"Wheeell," Bay said cheerily. "Best make a plate, then. The turkey is excellent."

The remainder of dinner went on uneventfully. We made small-talk about my classes at Radix and their daily habits. On a couple of occasions I caught Stryde staring at me. He was so zoned out I doubted he heard a word of our conversation. I easily looked past it once I grasped how difficult everyday life was for him.

After dinner and a bit more conversation, Bay hugged me goodbye. There's no denying I relished it. Eiven patted me roughly on the back with a meaty hand and asked me to visit again soon.

"Goodbye," I said and stuck my hand out awkwardly to shake Stryde's. A lock of long black hair fell over his eyes when he looked down, bewildered, as if my arm had morphed into a groundhog. He may not have gotten the familial hair, but he had the eyes. The green orbs shot wildly back and forth to mine before he looked down again.

"I… May I walk you home?" he asked stiffly.

"Sure," I said slowly. I had planned to trace back, but a short walk in the woods wouldn't hurt.

We walked in silence for a while. I enjoyed the small noises of the forest, though they were louder and more clear now that I had embraced my animal form. I could discern a rodent shuffling through nearby leaves, an owl shifting restlessly overhead.

"Have you enjoyed your education so far at the Root?" Stryde asked.

"I have. I'm having more difficulty grasping some parts of the curriculum than others, but overall I love it. I've learned so much already. Did you go? To Radix?"

"Not for long. I went until...well, until the fighting. When he captured my mom and dad I thought I could save them. I was stupid. Young. He just caught me, too."

"Your mother? I never knew. I'm so sorry, Stryde."

"Yes. She... She died in the fights after the… After."

He couldn't even say the words 'Steward Massacre.' At least I knew that my own mother was still alive somewhere. That she hadn't been killed during a battle she wanted no part of.

"Oh, Stryde," I said and hugged him, trying to communicate my sorrow and support through the gesture.

He didn't return the hug, but stood stiffly, hands at his sides. I stood back from him and thanked him for escorting me.

"Goodbye, Stella," he said with a brittle bow.

8

Stella Stonewall
Student Journal Entry #8
Logged via Pia
Monday, June 30

I've just returned from dinner with my newfound fam…

"Pia?"

"Yes, Stella?"

"Is this journal private?"

"In what way do you mean?"

"I mean," I said, and rolled my eyes. "Is what I write in my Student Journal kept between you and I, or is it uploaded to some Radix cloud somewhere? Is there a chance that someone besides you and I read it?"

"Oh, there's always a chance of that, Stella. Best not write down what you don't want seen. But you know that."

"Mph," I grunted, suddenly nervous. "So, are you saying that anything I've written in my Student Journals already isn't private? That it's subject to inspection or something?"

"I do not think there's anyone out there scouring Student Journals for deets on your love life, if that is what you mean."

"That is not what I mean." I huffed out an agitated breath. "Why the hell isn't what I write in my journal private? And did you really just say 'deets?'"

"It's a Student Journal, Stella. Not your super secret diary."

"You really get on my nerves sometimes." I made a face at Pia, fully aware that I was conducting an argument with an electronic device.

"Is that so?" she replied. "I think you are just a peach!"

"Is that sarcasm, Pia?" *Maybe I could* accidentally *drop her in the toilet.*

"Affirmative. What is your concern, Stella? Is there something you wish to keep secret?"

"Oh. Ah, no. That last journal entry just included some things I'm self-conscious about, that's all. No big deal."

I breathed deeply and prayed for patience. It was totally a big deal. I had laid out a first-hand account of the existence and continued transgressions of the Drakontos dragons. On top of that, I had stated very clearly that I possessed a dragon form. I revised the old entry at once, hoping against hope that nothing had or ever would come of it.

9

"Who sent you flowers?" Gresham asked when he picked me up from my room at Sabre Hall.

At his question, the tiniest of pangs plucked my little heart.

"Oh. I don't know," I said. "No message, just my name on the card."

His brows drew together in disapproval. "No idea who sent them?"

"No. I…ah… I really thought they were from you."

"Hmph," was all he said.

Aemon Lochlain lived just outside of town in a small craftsman-style cottage. I had expected him, a small person, to live in a proportional home, but his could have housed any family. He welcomed Gresham and I into a den that at some time over the last century had drowned in books and papers. Though we were expected, he nonetheless scraped piles from a sofa to accommodate us.

"I made tea," he announced as he rounded the corner with a brass tray. The contents rattled and clanked as he looked over his glasses, scouring the sitting room for a flat surface.

"Thank you, Professor Lochlain," I said as he sloshed my tea into a ceramic cup. His small hands made every regular-sized thing he handled seem colossal by comparison. It was difficult not to stare, so I forced my attention to the titles of books strewn about the room.

Once he'd filled his and Gresham's cups half full he hefted a bottle of golden-colored liquid and topped the two off before offering it to me.

"Oh… Ah… Thank you. What is it?"

"What is it? Drambuie, child, of course." His thick brows knit in disapproval.

Gresham must have seen the incomprehension on my face. "Drambuie is a liqueur made from Scotch, heather honey, and spices," he said. "It's a delicacy here from your world. Try it. You'll never see tea the same."

"All righty." I nodded my approval before adding a dollop of Drambuie to my own cup with great ceremony.

Scotch had never been my thing. I know I would be a lot more cultured and refined if it was, but to me it was like liquid fire. And maybe that's the point.

But Drambuie…dangerous. It warmed me from the inside out, like tiny fuses had been wired from my belly to my extremities, and when those fuses were ignited the liquid fire ran the length of my body. Instant comfort. I breathed a bit easier, relaxed just a notch.

Perfect. Just perfect for a serious conversation with a scholarly gnome and my enigmatic older lover about my fate as a wolf-dragon love child.

Professor Lochlain—I had never received permission to call him Aemon—clasped the arms of a green suede chair with knobby fingers before hefting onto an ottoman and backing into the seat with a grunt. "Stella, Gresham has told me what happened at the crater. Your wolf. Your dragon. Your discovery that you're an omni."

My stomach bottomed out before rolling into a hard knot at his casual declaration of my circumstances. I didn't speak; didn't know where to start. When I began to fidget Gresham cut in. "Aemon is a trusted friend, Stella. He and I have worked together to find you from the beginning."

"I know," I squeaked and took a long breath before directing my attention at the gnome. "Professor Lochlain, Gresham told me you're wise and level-headed and will be a great resource in determining my way forward. This is all just very difficult. And terrifying."

"Aye, I know it is," he said with a sympathetic nod. "But we're here to help you. And to do that, we need to lay all of our cards on the table. We must try to consider the facts without bias so we avoid mistakes. The more honest you are with yourself, and the more realistic we are about your situation, the better this will all work out in the end. The road ahead is going to be tough for you, Stella, but we'll help you find your way."

"Thank you," I croaked, both gratitude and fear producing a lump in my throat.

"Don't thank me yet, child. We've a ways to go." He took a long sip of his doctored tea before continuing. "Now, let's first consider the primary problem: public perception as it relates to your safety. We know that the public fear of dragons, any dragon, is visceral and not linked to rationale. Certainly anyone that knows you understands you would never be a threat to Thayer."

I nodded, pleased by his synopsis of my character. "My thoughts, exactly. Can't we just tell people, show them that I'm not a danger? That I didn't grow up in Thayer and had no knowledge or interaction with those dragons that attacked?"

He sucked a breath before twisting his mouth in regret. "I'm afraid publicizing you're an outsider is probably not the best course of action right now. And as to you not having contact with the Drakontos dragons, well, that's not exactly true, now is it?" His glance turned pointed. "Edina, the most infamous and feared of the dragons, raised you."

"Yes, but..but" I sputtered. "She wasn't Edina Drakontos. I knew her as Elena Stonewall. I'd never even heard her real name until a few weeks ago. I sure never knew she had such a horrifying history."

"Further," he said as he cocked a furry eyebrow, "you recently freed three of the dreaded Drakontos, who willingly endured humiliating mutilation at the hands of Brandubh rather than betray you."

"No." I groaned and shook my head. "It's not like that. In the end they helped Brandubh set me up anyway, despite having their wings clipped."

"I know that," he said. "And you know that. Gresham, too. But everyone else will see you as one more dragon with very close ties to Thayer's most hated enemies."

"You know what I don't understand?" I said, my voice rising with each word. "Dragons didn't kill people. Brandubh killed people. He's the one who enslaved the dragons, he's the one who manipulated them and used them as his own personal weapons of mass genocide. The Drakontos were victims, too."

"And now she's a dragon sympathizer," Lochlain said and nodded smugly to Gresham.

"Oh, screw you," I spat before I remembered I was working for a letter grade from the gnome. At that moment, I didn't care that he was my teacher. "Why haven't you people been able to find and prosecute Brandubh? He's the real enemy, and you know it. You've had hundreds of years, but he's still out there and here we sit, trying to establish a defense to something I haven't even done. What exactly am I guilty of? Being born? If you two hadn't sought me out and dragged me here, I wouldn't be facing this nightmare in the first place."

Gresham's jaw ticked with irritation, with anger. As Thayer's director of defense, he was certainly the man who shouldered the responsibility for Brandubh's extended freedom.

Professor Lochlain's weathered face held a goofy grin as he looked back and forth between me and Gresham. I suspected that he had provoked me to anger in order to see if I would defend the dragons, and I'd played right into his hands.

"I get your point, Professor," I conceded. "I'll never be seen as unbiased. I'll never be trusted." I couldn't help but add a mumbled, "Even though I'm right."

He nodded and picked the conversation back up before Gresham and I lost our tempers. "The unknown here is Brandubh, of course. In addition to being seen as a dragon, a dragon sympathizer, and an outsider, as long as he's still on the loose you'll be viewed as vulnerable to his machinations, just like your mother and her family."

"But I'm not. I proved that when I was able to change to wolf and attack him."

"Exactly. I've given this some thought, and I have come up with a two-pronged offense." Professor Lochlain used the chair arms to push himself back in the worn seat. "First," he ticked a finger, "pursuing the dissemination of knowledge that you inherited your father's thayerenthropy is key. We must show people that you have multiple forms…before they discover that one of them is a dragon."

"Thayerenwha?" I asked.

"Thayerenthropy." He grunted his disapproval of my ignorance. "It means, literally, mankind of Thayer. As people who can manipulate any form, omnis are known to be the most evolved of us."

Oh, wait'll I tell my friends I'm so evolved, I thought and let out a hysterical giggle. Gresham's gaze shot to mine conspicuously, and I worked to wipe off the grin and sit up straight.

"Okay," I said at the same time Gresham added, "Yes, Aemon, very good." He turned to me. "I can help you with that."

"Okay. That's a start. What's the second prong in your plan?" I asked.

"You must come out strongly against the Drakontos dragons. You must condemn their heinous and violent history. And when you help Gresham capture them, I believe, the Thayerian public will no longer see you as a threat, but as a valued citizen."

"When I *what*?" I screeched.

"Wait, Stella," Gresham interceded with a sharp look in Professor Lochlain's direction. "This is something we can discuss in the future. When things are clearer. When you've had time to sort out your feelings about your mother and the other dragons."

I jerked my arm from Gresham as he tried to calm me. "I'm never going to help you capture them, Gresham. You can forget that right now. Could you promise me they'd get a fair trial? That the truth of their role in the Steward Massacre would come out and be seen objectively?"

When he said nothing I knew he couldn't. So this was their plan. For me to betray my own blood. My stomach roiled with disgust at the thought of assisting in the capture of my newfound family.

I was so mad I could've breathed fire. And I really thought I might. I had to calm down. Or get out of there. Or both. My heart thundered at such a pace I decided calming down was the first priority.

"Can I use your restroom?" I blurted in the general direction of Professor Lochlain.

"Of course," he said, startled at my biting tone. "Just through there."

I pushed open the creaky bathroom door and tripped on a wooden stool that sat just under the sink. I let out a string of curse words as my shoulder hit the hard wall.

"I'm all right," I announced to deter them from coming to check on me.

I splashed cold water on my face and made an effort to slow my erratic breathing. My head throbbed in time to my racing heart, so I leaned against the wall and took several deep breaths to regain my composure. It was when my heart finally slowed, when the ringing stopped in my ears, that I caught parts of Gresham and Lochlain's muted conversation.

I couldn't catch what Gresham had said, but Professor Lochlain was less discreet. "How did Gaspare react when you told him she's his own niece?"

My breath hitched on its way down my diaphragm and it was a struggle not to cough to better hear Gresham's reply. It was faint.

"He wants to meet her, of course, though I'm hesitant for obvious reasons."

"I imagine she wants to meet her father's people, too," Professor Lochlain said. "That could certainly help with the first portion of our plan—a unified front. Gaspare could make a show of teaching her the ways of an omni."

"I haven't told her," Gresham mumbled.

Lochlain gasped. "You haven't told her?"

"Quiet," Gresham rasped.

It was too late. The ringing in my ears was back. Worse, darkness crept around the edges of my vision. I knew what came next: stars. I was on the verge of passing out. Damned if I would do it in Professor Lochlain's squatty bathroom.

10

Unconsciousness crept toward me like a man with a burlap sack. Before it could overtake me, I raised the back of one foot, hoping the movement and the thought of my Sabre Hall room was enough to get me home. It was. I fell roughly onto my bed before everything went dark.

"Stell? Stella? Gods help me," Timbra's frantic words were far away. They echoed and bounced within my brain long before I was able to make sense of where I was, what had happened.

I sat up with a jolt as adrenaline coursed through my veins at the recollection of the whispered revelations just before I passed out.

I found Timbra's gaze. "How long was I out?"

Her face was flushed with concern. "What's going on? What's wrong?" She lay her hands on my forehead and my cheeks, checking for a temperature, before I knocked them away.

"How long was I unconscious? It's important. I need to hurry."

"Ah, I don't know. Maybe a minute at most? I heard you moan and the bed springs creak. I started to leave you to your business, but when it became eerily quiet, I knew something wasn't right. You're fairly loud…"

"Okay, I get the point. Next time, I'm getting a suite mate who's deaf."

"Oh!" she said, affronted. "Like who? You want to share a shower with a snake?"

"Dammit. Let's debate my new accommodations later. I need to know who can create a ward around my room. Fast."

"What? Why?"

"Now! Who's the best at wards?"

"Emrynne. She's just down the hall." I was out the door and running to the end of the hall before she finished the sentence. Emrynne Brecker was weird as hell, but rumored to be very talented. Her door was embellished with glitter, and fragrant flowers that I suspected were real.

The evidence of her expertise in ward-making hit me like a dog to an electric fence. I lifted my arm to knock on her door and suffered a charge so forceful it knocked me back two feet. And hurt like hell. I looked to the ceiling for patience, but found none. I needed help fast, before Gresham and Professor Lochlain realized I was gone.

"Emrynne," I hollered through the closed door. "Emrynne, I need your help with a ward. I'm in a bit of a hurry."

I heard shuffling inside, but the door never opened. Timbra caught up with me and smartly stayed clear of the door's wards.

"What'll you give me?" a high, thin voice called from inside.

"Give you? What? What do you mean?"

"If you need this urgent help—*my* urgent help—I expect some form of payment. What'll you give me?"

Oh hell. Everyone was wasting my precious time. I had to find a way to keep Gresham from tracing to my room, and fast, so I could buy time to think. I didn't know what he and Lochlain were planning, but it was obvious they'd kept something from me. Obvious Gresham, that cold bastard, was keeping secrets from me. Again. I knew I was right not to trust him. Damn, damn, damn. Damn, I was an idiot.

"What do you have in mind, Emrynne?" She was angling for something.

"I want to meet your friend. The one I see you with at the bar. The big one."

"Boone?" I quirked a brow at Timbra. "You know he and Timbra are together, right?"

"Not that oaf!" she called. "The one who looks like he could set a girl on fire just by looking at her long enough," Her voice took on a dreamy sigh quality. "Brown curls. Endless dark eyes."

"Ewan?" *Does she really think she has a shot with him? Whatever. Not my concern; I'm in a hurry.* "Fine. I'll introduce you to Ewan."

Timbra elbowed me hard in the shoulder. "What?" I mouthed. Timbra mimed the universal sign for 'She crazy.' I shrugged. I didn't have a lot of options.

"When?" Emrynne asked through the door.

"What?" I was beyond irritated with Girl Crazy.

"When will you introduce me to Ewan?"

"Oh, for god's—tonight. We'll go down to the bar tonight. Okay? I need help fast. Let's go now!"

She opened the door with a flourish and stepped into the hall. Without a word she fluttered toward my room, her flowing white dress and long blond hair trailing behind her.

Emrynne was beautiful, of that there was no doubt. Perhaps she was best described as "ethereal." She had some kind of magic princess thing going on, complete with a glowing aura. In Thayer, "normal" was a really big tent. When people descended of dragons, of lions, of wolves, the boundaries of conventional were wide…and blurred. Emrynne eclipsed even those.

Today, though, that magical something about her was to my own advantage.

"Who, or what, are you trying to ward against?" she asked, all business.

"I want to keep someone out. Someone who's been in my room before."

"Does he or she mean you harm?"

"No—yes—I don't know. I think my opinion and his on what's in my best interest may be at odds. How about that?"

"Fine. Let's ward against this specific person."

"Actually, can I ward against anyone coming in my room? Except Timbra?"

"You expecting trouble?" she asked with a smirk.

"No," I lied. "I just don't like the idea of people popping in and out of my personal space. I should've done this sooner, truthfully."

"Yes, you should. You'll learn. That's why we're all here at The Root."

"Did I say yet that I was in a hurry?" I yelled this last, and she clamped her mouth shut with a scowl.

Emrynne stood in the center of my room and instructed Timbra and I to sit quietly on my bed while she performed the necessary ritual. She began with her eyes closed, her slender arms hanging limply to her sides. She extended only her hands so they formed a right angle to her arms—like a Roaring 20s flapper would. Concentration creased her forehead as the hairs of my arms stood up in recognition of power evoked. It was weighty, earthy, nearly oppressive.

With the grace of a ballet dancer, she arced her arms above her head in one smooth motion, her hands still bent at right angles. I risked a look at Timbra to see if she, too, felt the magical undertones in the room. She did. Her over-large eyes bulged in distress.

Still breathing deeply, Emrynne had lay her head back, and appeared to be pushing something toward the sky. She abruptly arced her arms back down to her sides and I felt, like a ripple through my being, the protective magic encompass me, Timbra, and the confines of my room.

Emrynne stood for a moment breathing, relaxing, releasing the tension that she had built in order to form the ward.

With one last breath she opened her eyes and smiled at me. "There," she said. "Nothing to it. See you at the bar at eight."

She left without a backward glance.

"What the hell was all that about? What's going on?" Timbra fumed the moment Emrynne was gone.

I had a decision to make. Should I tell all to Timbra, my trusted friend, and hope that her love for me overrode a life-long fear and hatred of dragons? I wanted so desperately to tell her. I yearned to unload my burden, to have someone that I trusted know my darkest secret, and to accept me anyway.

I opened my mouth to start from the beginning when I felt a pull on my consciousness. It was as if my mind was a ball of rubber bands and someone had tugged the outermost one. It plucked within my brain, and my eyes watered at the sensation. I shook my head to clear it.

"Stella?" Timbra's voice was strained. "Stella, what now?"

"I—I think Gresham is trying to trace here. To my room. Only it's warded and he's being rejected. Emrynne must've wired the ward to me somehow. I really need to learn how to do th—ow!" The plucking went on for several more seconds before it stopped. That's when I heard Gresham roaring at me from the bottom floor.

"Stella!" he called from the stairwell. I gasped and looked at Timbra, whose eyes were wide as she shook her head in confused denial.

"Stella!" Gresham yelled. "You warded against me? Let me in. Now!"

No way was that happening. Maybe if I ignored him he'd go away.

"*Ste-lla*!" he roared, and his resonant voice ricocheted off of every wall and corner.

People had begun to stick their heads out of the doors of their rooms. It was urgent I shut the situation down fast.

"Lovers' quarrel," I called down the halls. "Can't get enough of this."

Most of my neighbors rolled their eyes, but a few gave doubtful smirks. Assholes.

To Gresham I yelled, "This ain't no damned *Streetcar Named Desire*, Gresham. Go. Away!"

"I need to speak to you," he grated. "Urgently. I know what you overheard. I can explain."

"You'll have to explain it to all of Sabre Hall, then, 'cause I've warded you from my room."

"You know I can't do that," he said, his voice rough with increasing fury before he gave in to his temper and bellowed, "Come down here!"

From the corner of my eye I spotted Ewan charging down the hall like metal to a magnet. "What's going on, Stella? What's he yelling about?"

"We're having a disagreement. He wants to talk about it. I don't. I've warded him from my room." Close enough to the truth, anyway.

Ewan's eyes lit with anticipation at the opportunity to rumble with Gresham. His grin was dark and mischievous before he took on a more resolute expression and nodded once. "I'll handle it," he said, and strode away.

"What happened then?" Mari asked, her eyes shiny with astonishment. Her strawberry blond hair was whipped into a ponytail that swished wildly as she served her patrons. She was waitressing *and* participating in our conversation. After tending her responsibilities her small but curvy body smoothly maneuvered back to our table each time.

"Then I said, 'Mr. Gresham, you heard the lady. I think she prefers that you *fuck off*.'"

"You did not," I scoffed, though I knew he had. We'd heard every strained word of Gresham and Ewan's encounter. We could have even without super hearing. Their growled exchange rumbled through Sabre Hall like thunder reverberating along a riverbank.

"I did," Ewan said. "And I swear his hands twitched with the desire to choke me. Ha! I wish he'd tried. After that he left, nearly blowing the door off its hinges."

"You better be glad he didn't take you on, wolf," scoffed Boone. "You don't stand a chance against him. Not to mention the fact he's got a whole department of badass behind him. You're just…well…you."

"Oh! Speaking of which," I yelped, "why didn't one of you tell me about his day job?"

"What do you mean?" asked Layla after a swallow of her drink. "What's he do?"

"He's Thayer's director of defense," Timbra announced with weight.

"So you did know," I accused.

"Well, sure. I thought you did, too. It honestly never struck me that you wouldn't. I mean, everyone knows him. Being a Cabinet member is fairly prestigious. Then again, you're not from here... Um…sorry?"

"Didn't you wonder why the Director of Thayerian Defense was giving a nobody like me the grand tour?"

"I did," she said. "I asked several times, if you'll recall."

"What *is* his interest in you, Stella?" Ewan had whittled down to the pith of the issue.

And here we were again. I was in the position of telling all or lying to my friends.

If I'd learned anything from the recent mess with Gresham it was that I couldn't be too careful where I placed my trust. Could I trust anyone at all? Increasingly, I felt the answer was no.

"Hello, Stella," called a confident, sing-song voice. Emrynne moved through tables toward us, her blond hair swishing just under her butt as she walked. She had changed into a lavender goddess-dress that amplified her etherealness to damn-near radiating love and light. It could escape no one's notice that her halter top wasn't halting much.

I had forgotten the deal we'd made. *Damn.* I felt terrible about the situation I put Ewan in, but when I turned to explain I concluded he wouldn't mind too much. His eyes were firmly affixed to two peach-sized swells shimmying beneath lavender chiffon.

I cleared my throat to attract his attention. No response. I cleared it with more force, and he turned to me with a distracted, "Hmm?"

"Ewan, this is Emrynne. She lives on my floor. I invited her to have a drink with us tonight."

"Oh…ah…yes. Hello," he said and stood. She proffered her hand as if he would kiss it, but his intention was clearly to shake it. The result was awkward, limp. "I've seen you around The Root," he said, "though I don't believe we've met."

"No, we haven't. I'm so happy to finally meet you," she gushed as a delicate pink flushed her high cheekbones.

I introduced her to everyone else at the table, and she inclined her head to each before turning eagerly back to Ewan, who I thought went to great lengths to make her feel at home.

After a while I slipped back into my own thoughts, turning both old and new revelations, and my potential options, over in my head.

'*How did Gaspare react when you told him she's his own niece?*' Lochlain had said. I was certain they were referring to me. Who was Gaspare? I had an uncle? Did that mean my father had a brother? Other family? Had they known about me? Tried to find me? No. Gresham and Lochlain's conversation indicated my pedigree was a surprise to everyone.

'*I imagine she wants to meet her father's people*,' he'd said. Damn right I did. But I knew nothing about someone named Gaspare, or even where to start looking.

'*He wants to meet her, though I'm hesitant for obvious reason*s.' The reasons Gresham might be hesitant were not obvious to me. I needed more information.

"I haven't forgotten that something suspicious is going on with you and Gresham," Ewan whispered roughly in my ear. I shivered, less at his words than his tone, which indicated he wouldn't stop until he was satisfied he knew every detail of the day's altercation.

"It's none of your business," I whispered back and turned from him to discourage any further inquiry.

"The hell it isn't." He yanked my chair so that I faced him again. "You're my business, whether you like it or not. And stop trying to fix me up with Emrynne. With anyone. I don't need your help when it comes to women."

"Yeah, I noticed," I grumbled.

"Good. Keep your nose out of my bed. Unless you want to be the one in it, in which case you're welcome any time."

11

My cheeks heated at the brazen invitation. My brain short-circuited and I couldn't form a response, though other parts of me had responded. I could so clearly imagine being in his bed, his big body rising over mine with the forceful confidence that manifested in everything he did. For a few naughty moments I allowed the fantasy to go on, imagining the feel of his rough hands reaching beneath—

Ewan was the one clearing his throat for attention this time. I glanced away in an attempt to regain my composure. *What are you thinking, Stonewall?* I shook my head to clear it. I shouldn't be having such thoughts when I was involved with Gresham. Well, actually, I probably wasn't involved with Gresham anymore. I was fairly sure *that* ship had not just sailed, but had crashed into the rocky cliffs of secrecy and betrayal.

As I accepted the development, realized the loss of Gresham, I waited for my heart to break.

Waited.

But it never did.

Was I furious that he'd kept things from me yet again? Yes. Humiliated that I was so naïve as to think Gresham had my best interests at heart? Mm. Hmm. Supremely ashamed that I'd been so stupid? You betcha. But heartbroken? No.

And that didn't surprise me. I was Stella Stonewall, after all. Never did a girl possess a more befitting name. At twenty-two I had yet to be in love. My boyfriends over the years had always complained that I was "unemotional." I had a history of breaking things off when someone was headed for heartbreak, and that someone was never me. But…I wasn't opposed to love; I'd just never known it.

I'd never loved Gresham. I was attracted to him, had come to depend on him, to appreciate his knowledge and experience, to like and respect him. He was *red hot* in the sack. But love was never a consideration, and thank god for that. All the better to get over him.

But just because I wasn't heartbroken over Gresham didn't mean I should hop right into a relationship with someone else. No. This thing with Gresham was a lesson learned the hard way. And I had always been a good student.

I came crashing back to the present when Emrynne said, "Next time, Stella, you can create your own damn wards." She put as much force in her words as her willowy little body could muster. Though the actual effect was as intimidating as a good scolding from a kitten, I nonetheless felt guilty. She'd heard Ewan's reprimand…and his offer.

"Good luck with *that*," my faithful and supportive friend Timbra muttered from the side of her mouth.

To Timbra I shot a discreet "Good luck with *this*" finger. To Emrynne I gave an apologetic look. "Thanks again for your help." It was the only thing I could say as she stomped away.

Mari's shift at Sabre Bar was over, and after a few minutes she and Layla left us in favor of some time alone.

"Stella, we all know something serious is going on with you," Boone said abruptly after the two had gone.

"Yes, what was all that about with Gresham today?" asked Timbra. "You didn't just have a fight; you were afraid to be near him. And you were unconscious when I found you in your room."

Ewan went deathly still beside me. "Did he hurt you, Stella?" he breathed.

I tried to formulate an explanation of the situation in my head, but none came. Silence went on longer than intended, and Ewan's body—no, his aura—began to fracture. He had taken my silence to mean that Gresham *had* harmed me, and he was so angry he was at risk of changing to his animal form right there in the bar.

"Oh, shit. Ewan. No! He didn't touch me."

But he was so far gone he didn't hear my words. A snarl escaped lips that had retracted to reveal elongating teeth. Sharp teeth. He needed to calm down. Fast.

I didn't think. I closed in on him, my nose a breath away from his as I held his face in my hands.

"Get back, Stella!" Boone bellowed and reached across the table for me.

I didn't move. Timbra held Boone back and took a gentler approach to our enraged friend. "Stella, back away from the wolf," she said. "He doesn't have control of himself right now. He could hurt you without intending to. Just back away and let's all cool down," she soothed.

"He's not going to hurt me." I was confident of the fact like I was confident I'd meet the stars each night I looked up to find them.

Ewan Bristol could never harm me. I sat up taller to meet his eyes. He was so on edge that their chocolate depths darted continuously to each corner of the room. Growled sentence fragments escaped with each exhale.

"Ewan." I called his name with confidence, but when it was clear he hadn't heard me I began to plead. "Ewan? Can you look at me?"

He snarled again, his fingers clenching into tight fists, his body vibrating with repressed rage.

"Ewan? Ewan, please?" I whispered.

He finally swung his eyes down to me. They softened ever so slightly, and pent-up breaths around the room released at the likelihood Ewan would recover.

"He didn't hurt me, Ewan," I said. "He's been keeping some pretty big secrets from me is all, and I found out. Secrets about my family."

Ewan's chest expanded with his efforts to reclaim control of his body. He closed his eyes, released the breath, and when he opened them again they were back to the intelligent, impassioned ones I knew so well.

"Stella, we're your friends," Timbra said and lay a gentle hand on my arm. "We care for you deeply, and we know you feel the same. If there's a way we can help you, I wish you'd let us in. You know you can trust us. Deep down, you know you can."

My conscious mind screamed, "*Don't do it!*"

"All right," I breathed. "But not here." I raised away from Ewan, and my legs shook from the aftereffects of the tense little moment.

"We can" Ewan cleared his throat of wolf and tried again. "We can use my room. I've warded it for sound."

In Ewan's room we all found a comfortable place to sit or a door jamb on which to lean. At first Boone and Timbra made small talk so that it wasn't so obvious everyone in the room was waiting for me. Ewan made no such pretense. He stared openly at my mouth, as if he could will it to start moving.

I had no idea how I was going to say the very difficult things I needed to say. Best to get it over with, like ripping off a Band-Aid. I jumped right in and hoped I wasn't screwing it up.

"So, remember how I turned into a wolf at Solstice Fest and ran from those dragons?"

Three heads nodded.

"And you know last week I escaped Brandubh by turning into my wolf."

"Mm-hmm's" all around.

"Well, what you don't know is…as it turns out…well…Gresham knew my father. And apparently he was an omni."

Stunned silence protracted in the room. I searched each of their faces for some clue to what they were thinking. Timbra's mouth fell open in shock. Boone frowned with incomprehension, and Ewan's expression was disturbingly calculating.

"Damn," Boone said. "I did not see that coming."

"Stella, are you serious?" yelped Timbra, her fawn ears twitching with nervous excitement. The movement caught Boone's eye and a goofy grin spread across his face.

"So, that makes you an omni?" Ewan's eyes had reduced to slits. He squinted so long that I suspected he was trying to look within me. To my knowledge, that was not possible. At least I hoped not.

"So they say," I said casually. "Half, anyway."

"Who's 'they'?"

"Gresham and Professor Lochlain. I met with them earlier tonight. I overheard Lochlain ask Gresham how someone felt about having a niece. Said whoever it is wants to meet me. Lochlain thought it was a good idea. That this 'Gaspare' could teach me the ways of an omni."

"Gaspare?" gasped Timbra.

"That's what he said. Why? You know someone by that name?"

Boone was struck silent, a feat in itself, and Ewan had gone pale as the moon. He worked his throat several times, as if he couldn't swallow the information.

When he found his voice he asked, "Stella, did you learn your father's name?"

"I did." I nodded. "Gabrio. Gabrio Shaw."

"Good gods on a green bean," Timbra panted before slouching onto the bed.

Ewan shook his head in slow denial.

Boone's big lips, which until then hung open in shock, snapped closed. "So, you're saying that your uncle, the one Gresham and Lochlain said wanted to meet you, to teach you the ways of an omni…is Gaspare Shaw. Is that what you're saying?" He turned one ear toward me, his head listing to the side. Like if he just listened hard enough, the answer would be no.

But the answer was yes. "What the hell's going on, guys? Who is Gaspare Shaw?"

"And what of your father?" Ewan almost whispered. "Does he know of your existence, too?"

I had to be careful. I could only tell them so much. Nothing about my mother or her family. I wasn't ready to reveal the dragon angle. I might never be.

"I'm told my father died long ago."

"I'm sorry," Timbra and Boone put in at the same time.

I nodded my head in acknowledgment, but wouldn't be sidetracked. "Who's Gaspare Shaw, Ewan? Why are you all acting like it's a big deal?"

"Because it is a big deal, Stella. Gaspare Shaw is the most powerful person in Thayer."

"No," I scoffed, though the contents of my stomach threatened to make a reappearance.

"Oh, yes. If what they said is true, you're the prime minister's niece."

The blood drained from my own face and I ran a hand across my forehead, which was suddenly covered in a cold sweat. "No," I repeated. First my mother's loaded background and now this. My life could not possibly get any more complicated. The prime minister? Of Thayer? Surely this was all just a very bad misunderstanding.

I was so tired. Tired of questions, sick of surprises, and fed-the-eff-up with secrets and lies. I pressed the pads of my hands into my eyes and tried to force the bad news from the front of my mind.

"At least things are starting to make sense now," Ewan said. "This certainly explains Gresham's excessive interest in you."

"Excuse me?" I bristled and looked up.

He gave me an exasperated look. "Now we know why Gresham latched onto you, Stella. He works for Prime Minister

Shaw. He always has. Getting…close to you…was a way for him to keep tabs on you."

The sting of his words cut into me like a steel-tipped whip. "For your information, Ewan, we discovered who my father was only recently. He didn't know who my father was, who I was, only that I existed out there somewhere."

His uncompromising glare told me he didn't believe that for one minute. "And how did he know to go looking for you? Tell me again. I've forgotten."

Ewan Bristol forgot nothing. I eyed him. Stood up straighter. "Dean Miles saw me in a vision. She told him what she'd seen, gave him a name. She foresaw that Gresham and I would become…involved."

He grunted and his nostrils flared. "And how fortuitous that her vision became reality."

"Don't go there again, Ewan," I said. "We've already been through this. Mine and Gresham's relationship is none of your business. Don't say something out of jealousy you'll regret."

"Jealousy?" Ewan balked, his bold eyes on fire with emotion. "It's not jealousy that I feel about it, Stella. It's anger. It's profound outrage that he took something that belongs to me. And righteous indignation that you gave it away."

I was stunned silent at the truth behind his words. He meant it. Flutters of forbidden pleasure scrambled up my spine and filled me with a sick satisfaction. It was a visceral response to his bold claim. Damn him.

"It doesn't matter now, Ewan," I said. "It's over. I—"

"Damn right it's over," he cut me off. I cut him an eye.

"I need to decide what to do next," I said. "I don't feel like I can trust Gresham anymore. He's kept too many secrets from me. Too many secrets *about* me."

"I think so too, Stella," said Timbra. "We can all at least agree that his motives may not have been pure. Sure, he may have meant well, and…I could be wrong, but I don't think he set out to hurt you. The fact remains, though, that he works for Shaw. And if Shaw knows about you, I expect it'll be no time before he finds you."

Boone's wholesome face was covered with a deliberative mask. "Wait a minute," he said slowly. "Did I miss the part when we talked about your mother? If this Gabrio Shaw was your father, how did he meet your mother in another world?"

I couldn't form words. My throat closed in fear and my pulse raced as I searched for a way out of the line of questioning. I didn't want to lie to my friends. I didn't. But I couldn't reveal my mother's identity. It was bad enough Gresham and Lochlain knew. And Gresham had proved highly untrustworthy. I hoped it wouldn't result in disaster for me.

It was Timbra who came to my rescue. "Stella's mother always refused to discuss her father," she said. "Stella doesn't know anything about their relationship."

Boone shook his head in sympathy. "And with your father dead, you may never know. I'm sorry."

12

"Stella, girl, stop gnawing your cuticles. It'll be all right. We'll figure this out."

Timbra eyes were filled with empathy as she watched me fidget in my chair during our Wednesday morning Intro to Craft class. For once the stand-in professor, Dean Miles, was the least of my concerns. She never missed an opportunity to humiliate me or make me feel inadequate in some way. Honestly, I would've welcomed the distraction.

My smile at Timbra's ever-forward way of navigating life was weak, but that wasn't her fault. I was feeling significantly less positive about the situation.

"I just don't know what to do next," I said.

"Too bad you can't divine some kind of plan or see the future through a spell or something," she mused.

"Timbra, that's it!" I yelped.

"What's it?" She blinked her over-long eyelashes.

"Obviously, I need help. And this place is crawling with clairvoyants, oracles, and seers of all kinds. I don't know what to do, but surely someone could help me see the right path. Right?"

"Sure, I guess. Who do you think could help?"

"Hell, I don't know. I'm new here. Don't you know anyone?"

"I'm afraid my family's not very magical. We excel more in the political arena. But I did hear our Elements professor saying she dabbled in pyro-osteomancy."

"Pyro-what?"

"It's a kind of divination that uses bones heated over a fire until they crack. Then someone reads the cracks to foretell the future."

"What kind of bones?" I yelped. *Ew.*

"I dunno. Surely animal. I don't think it has to be the pinkie toe of a virgin or anything."

"Wait a minute," I said slowly. "Layla. Layla once said her mother is a clairvoyant. A good one."

"*Miss Ston-ewall?*" rang a sarcastically-pert sing-song voice.

Dean Miles. Perfect. "Yes?" I squeaked.

"I was just discussing how modern perceptions of witchcraft in other cultures are a convergence of science, superstition, and history. But you know that, of course, because you were listening so intently."

"Yes, ma'am."

"Tell me, Miss Stonewall, your particular thoughts on that image we're all so familiar with of a cone-hatted witch riding a broom across a moonlit night. I'm sure your perspective is one we'd all love to hear."

I knew she was being sarcastic, that she was taunting me, but what were my options at that point?

"Ah...okay." I cleared my throat. "Well, as early as the 1300s there's evidence that people who practiced witchcraft made compounds—hallucinogenic compounds—from plants like nightshade, henbane, mandrake.

"And a natural progression of drug use has pretty much always been to discover how to get higher faster. These people discovered their compounds could be absorbed through sweat glands like the armpit or mucus membranes like...well, farther south.

"Of course the primary benefit of these alternate routes was they bypassed the metabolizing function of the liver." I paused to aide my dry mouth with a swallow. The subject matter had made me uncomfortable. "Ah, so, they bypassed the liver and stayed higher longer. Not to mention avoiding a righteous stomachache.

"Anyway," I said, growing ever more agitated as I went on, "it's documented that the compounds were applied with the end of a broomstick." The room was dead silent, and the sound of my throat clearing was like a trumpet blast. "Ah, you get the point. And as for the flying…well…yeah. Middle-Aged version of an acid trip."

My classmates, who until then had sat in stunned disbelief, or morbid curiosity—maybe both—erupted in raucous laughter. I shrugged and swung an arm behind me before taking a little bow.

"Enough for today," Dean Miles clipped out. A wicked grin pushed her mouth toward her cruel eyes. Despite the applause, she was distinctly pleased she'd forced me to publicly discuss broomsticks stuck in hairy places.

Timbra shook her head in astonishment as we made our way across campus. "How could you possibly know that?"

"About the hallucinogens and the brooms, you mean?"

"Of course that's what I mean! Is it true?"

"I don't know if it's true or not. But I read about it in my extracurricular studies. Makes sense, though."

"Phew," she said and splayed fingers in front of her face. "Mind blown."

13

Layla's family lived in…well, a tree house. She traced Timbra and I to her family home after our morning classes. She was certain her mother wouldn't mind helping me, though she warned me she never worked for free. I didn't have a lot of money since I was living on a stipend, but I took what little cash I had. I hoped it would be enough.

The suspended wood cabin lay hidden deep in the forest among ancient trees. The tree that served as the foundation for Layla's home was the largest I'd ever seen. As we approached, it loomed bigger and bigger, its massive branches extending into the surrounding canopy and disappearing altogether.

The house itself was composed of smaller, rough logs, but featured modern windows and architecture. I spotted solar panels atop the slanted metal roof. What I didn't see was a logical way to the front door.

"How do we get in?" I asked Layla.

"By invitation only," she smirked.

"What does that mean?" Timbra's head tilted in question before it was jerked back by the force of motion. There was only a moment to consider what had caused her sudden jolt before I, too, began moving. And not of my own will.

When tracing, the sensation is akin to being exposed to a dark room full of dry ice. This was similar, but not the same. We were pulled through a cold, windy corridor, and I could do nothing to stop it. I tried to fight the forceful pull, first physically and then mentally, but I was powerless against it. Layla's dim words drifted toward me, "Don't freak. It's my mom. Just go with it."

Right.

In the end, I might as well have just gone with it, because there was no stopping Valdete Avenatio. We were vacuumed from the forest floor right into the family room of the tree house, where a woman with deep black hair stood with her hands on her hips.

Layla ran and caught her up in a tight hug. "Mom, hi, I've missed you," she gushed and placed a soft kiss high up on her mother's cheek. Layla was maybe the least-affectionate friend I'd made since coming to Thayer, so the sweet gestures took me by surprise. Layla often said she "wasn't cut out to deal with people," and generally lived up to the self-assessment. But to her mom she was adorably affectionate. "These are my friends from The Root, Stella Stonewall and Timbra Redfern."

"Ms. Redfern." Mrs. Avenatio's coiled hair bounced along her shoulders as she acknowledged Timbra. "I know your father from council meetings, of course," she said.

Her face crinkled in a somewhat remorseful look. "I'm sorry about the rough landing. Only way in or out of this place, though—by my invitation."

"Yes, ma'am," Timbra said. "No problem. I'm pleased to meet you, and thank you for welcoming us into your lovely home."

"Oh, don't ma'am me, for goodness sake. Call me Val. Please."

"Yes, ma'am—Val," said Timbra.

Val cut her eyes in my direction and the nearly-black orbs searched my face as her head tilted from side to side. It was a very avian thing to do.

"You I don't know, though. Who are your parents, girl?"

"Ah, well, that's why we're here, Mom. Stella was raised on the other side—America, actually. Her mother is missing and her father until recently was unknown. Now she's learned that her father was an omni named Gabrio Shaw."

"Gabrio Shaw, you said?" Val's face was inscrutable.

"Yes," I cut in. "Do you—did you know him?"

"I did meet him, yes. A long time ago. A fine man. Brave, strong. A bit foolhardy, but he was young. We all were. Who's your mother, then?"

"Elena Stonewall. She raised me alone. After my father was killed, I suppose."

"I don't know that name." She focused her beady eyes on me like a robin sighting a grub worm. "What can I help you with?"

Right to the point. Okay. "Well, you may have put together that if my father was Gabrio Shaw, then my uncle, of course, is Gaspare Shaw. I'm here because I don't know him, and I've suffered some fairly tough betrayals recently. I don't know who to trust or what to do. Is Gaspare a nice guy or some evil dictator from whom I should stay far away? Layla said you're a powerful clairvoyant. I want you to see my future. Specifically I want you to tell me if I should trust Gaspare Shaw."

"And what about Brandubh?" Val asked.

"What *about* Brandubh?" I asked, blinking in confusion.

"I know you're the girl that fought him. That somehow lived to tell about it. But I also know he's still out there. Don't you want to know if he'll seek you out again? Surely he came after you because of your lineage as an omni. You think he'll give up so easily if he has reason to want you?" She shook her head dubiously. "I don't."

She had assumed that Brandubh was after the heritage my father left me, rather than my mother. Fine by me.

"Oh, I know he'll be back," I said. "I have no doubt. And I want to be ready when he comes. But I could use some help. I know nothing about being an omni and they're apparently hard to come by. That's why I want to know if I can trust Gaspare. I want to know if going to him for help is a mistake."

"I see," Val said somberly. "Layla oversimplified my talents when she told you I was a clairvoyant. I'm an augur. Do you know what that means?"

I shook my head and looked to Timbra for help. She bunched her shoulders.

Val went on, "An augur divines the future by interpreting the flight patterns and the songs of birds. We are evolved of birds, the Avenatios, thus the connection."

My mouth formed an 'o,' but I didn't make a sound.

Val led the three of us away from her house along an old trail through the trees. As we traveled I was keenly aware of the ever-increasing volume of birds overhead. Val didn't appear to be calling them in any way, but they had progressively gathered and followed us.

"Your mother gave you a strong name," Val said, pulling me from my observation.

"What? Oh. Yes. I never minded the name Stella."

"Do you know what it means?" she asked.

"I do. It means "star" in Latin. Which is kinda awesome because I've always been drawn to the stars. I love astronomy."

"Names have power, Stella Stonewall. Remember that as you find your own way in this world."

"O-kay. Yes, ma'am, I will." *Whatever that meant.*

"Now, the birds divine what they will," she said as we stopped just inside the edge of the forest. Beyond lay a beautiful green meadow, its tall, thick grass rippling with the breeze. "I may ask them what we wish to know, but ornithomancy isn't an exact science. It's divination. It's open to the will of the powers that be. It's open to interpretation. And that's the beauty of it, really. We may not always know the right questions to ask, but the spirits always know the right answers."

I hadn't considered until that very moment that a clairvoyant—an augur—might be able to see more than what I asked for.

My palms broke out in a cold sweat. I swallowed convulsively, and my face and hands became clammy as I realized the possible repercussions. What if Val saw who my mother was, what she'd done? What if she saw my connection to Bay and the other Drakontos. *Oh, no, no, no*, I thought.

Surviving meant keeping my secrets.

The sound of the accumulated birds neared deafening, and I looked up to find the flock stirring. They were agitated. Ready for flight. Val squinted at me, suspicious of my reaction to her statement.

As she held my uneasy gaze, she flicked her hand and the birds took flight at once. The whole flock—hundreds of them—vaulted into the air. Their song wasn't sweet, and it wasn't pleasant. The birds screeched, cried, and dove roughly through tree limbs before exploding into the open meadow.

I took the opportunity to run.

My strategy was getting out of there before the birds showed Val who and what I was. Maybe some distance between from the flock would neutralize the effect.

But before I took two strides Val's firm grip was a vice around my upper arm. She clasped it so tightly I couldn't break free despite jerking with all my strength. She was stronger than she looked.

I tried to trace away, but she'd somehow prevented me from escaping.

"Still, girl," she said, though her thoughts were somewhere else entirely.

I wasn't going anywhere. My chin hit my chest as I hung my head in dread.

Val Avenatio watched intently as the birds ascended and swooped through the air, their wings extending and bracing against the airstreams to glide in a graceful dance with the wind. When the birds began calling she closed her eyes, concentrated on their song. I attempted to imagine what she might be interpreting from her avian cousins, but all I saw was a flock of squawking birds.

Timbra, who was prone to nervous energy already, was nearing over-stimulation. Her prone ears twitched furiously, instinct overriding her capacity for control. Timbra's eyes were wild, frantic, but she found the focus to shoot me a questioning look about Val's grip on my arm. I shrugged in resignation.

With an intake of breath so sharp she coughed to recover, Val's eyes shot open in alarm. She found my gaze immediately. "It's not possible," she breathed before whispering, "I knew her."

Origin Exposed

14

"You knew who?" I whispered, but I knew already.

"Your mother. Edina."

"Edina? No, Stella's mother was Elena, Ms. Avenatio," Timbra corrected.

I drew a soul-deep breath and exhaled it through strained lips. Then I just laid it all on the line.

"My mother changed her name, Timbra. Apparently she fled Thayer and raised me without ever revealing my true genesis—to me or anyone else."

"But, who was she then? The only Edina I ever heard of was the one they do re-enactments about at Solstice Fest—the dragon—" Timbra's words trailed off as her round eyes first held certainty, then doubt, and finally they seemed to plead with me not to admit it.

But there was no going back.

"My mother was Edina. The dragon."

I relayed the story to Timbra, Layla, and Val. How my mother had been tortured and abused by Brandubh. I told them how lovingly she had raised me, and that she was the kindest, gentlest soul I'd ever encountered. I begged them not to judge her by the horrific actions she was forced to make, and I tried to convince them that she was a victim, too.

"I knew her," Val said again. "Before."

"Was she as I knew her? Was she docile and meek?"

"On the contrary, she was fiery—pun intended," Val grinned and her black eyes gleamed. "She was fun and wild and free."

"I never knew her that way," I said, surprised by the loss I felt at the statement. "I think by the time she'd conceived me she'd had all of the "fire" tortured from her. The woman who raised me was gentle, but in truth she was just a shell."

"I'm sorry to hear that," Val said. "We were dear friends. We entered as primos together at The Root, and we were partners in Metamorphosis class since both our forms were airborne. Gods, we had such fun soaring the skies together." Small white teeth peeked from her lips when shot me a crooked grin. "Even though she dwarfed me."

"When the attacks began I didn't believe the stories about her. I knew my friend would never—could never—do such violent things. Then I saw it with my own eyes. I think she would have decimated me if I'd gotten in her way. Her actions were so incongruent with the girl I knew. I could never quite reconcile what went wrong. And I'm afraid many people—myself included—were biased against her due to her fearsome form."

"Like, 'that dragon didn't go crazy, that dragon went dragon'?" quipped Layla.

"Exactly," her mother said. "I'm afraid no one really stood up for the Drakontos, or any of the dragon families, once the attacks began. And how could they have? They'd have been annihilated just like the gnome and fae people."

"So, those dragons that were there in the crater when Brandubh attacked you?" Timbra asked.

"My grandmother, uncle, cousin."

"Damn." Layla said, and got it right.

"Did you help them escape?" Timbra asked weakly.

"No. I didn't. They simply got away."

"So," I asked Val to change the subject, "did you see anything else? Anything that can help me with Gaspare Shaw? Can I trust him? Should I go to him for help?"

"The path looked clear, though not unburdened, Stella. I saw him as a prominent figure in your future."

"Well, that's pretty vague, Val. Anything else? Anything I should avoid?"

"It's not an exact science, as I said. It is a gift, an art. But I did see that you aren't free of danger yet. You'll be betrayed yet again before all of this is through."

"Figures," I said. "Any idea who?"

She shook her head sadly and rubbed my back in a motherly way. "I wish I knew, hon. I wish I knew."

15

"Well, besides the freaky aviary show, that was a complete waste of time," I huffed and shoved my hair from my face after Timbra and I traced back to The Root.

"Oh, Stella," she admonished, "you know it wasn't. She gave you some direction. You can feel—well, kinda safe—about going to Prime Minister Shaw for help."

To my dubious look she sucked a breath through her straight square teeth and shrugged. Then she took on an expression so serious it seemed foreign on her sweet face. "You do realize that our conversation about your mother isn't over, right?"

Dread skittered across my back like a line of fire ants. I needed Timbra on my side. Besides her I didn't really *have* a side. That was not a conversation I was looking forward to. I abhorred the thought of her being frightened…or disappointed. Timbra Redfern's opinion of me meant a lot.

"I know, Timbra," I said. "Just promise me —"

She'd stopped listening to me. Her attention was focused across the lawn in the direction of Sabre Hall where a very large, very loud man shook his fist and pointed his finger at anyone stupid enough to stop and give him attention.

"What's *his* problem?" I mused as he transferred his anger from actual people to berate the shrubbery. I couldn't make out what he was saying but Timbra's cervid ears twitched wildly. She let out a long breath that sounded suspiciously like the word "shit." At the same time, Mr. Loud and Gnarly whipped his head in our direction. His eyes widened with recognition and he let out a bellow surely heard throughout the entire campus.

"Timbra Dawn Redfern!" he hollered, and both she and I ducked.

I looked to Timbra to see if she was in some sort of trouble. She was in trouble, all right. I could tell by the frantic look in her eyes that her mind was racing. Her normally tawny complexion had paled to an unnatural puce. She unwittingly took a step backward and I followed her lead. It was obvious she knew him. That he was pissed was even more apparent, but about what I sure as hell wasn't sticking around to find out. I clasped her hand, readying to trace and take her with me when she was suddenly jerked from my grasp. I looked up to find that the man had hold of Timbra's shoulder and was pushing her toward a small copse of trees.

"Hold the fuck on," I found the nerve to say. "Get your hands off her!"

"It's okay, Stella," Timbra said meekly as the man turned his ire toward me. "He's my father."

It was at this point that I noticed the ears—and the antlers. His ears were bigger than Timbra's; proportional to his broad body. But those *antlers*. My god he was menacing. Though covered in a gray-brown velvet because it was June, they were nonetheless one of the most extraordinary things I had set eyes on. They grew back from the top of his head before shooting out and upward into a comb-like structure at least four feet wide. The physics of how he remained standing upright was a mystery. The sheer neck and upper body strength it took to support those things was unfathomable. But he was definitely built for it. His thick chest held a bulk of muscle apparent even through his khaki button-down shirt.

My enthrallment must have been obvious because Timbra reprimanded him sharply. "Oh, put the antlers away, Father. You're scaring my friend."

"I'll do what I damn well please," he said, unable to control the volume of his words. "And you'll bite your tongue if you've got any sense left in your head. But if what I've been hearing is true, you either never had any to begin with, or it's been corrupted by your perverse sexual escapades."

Timbra jerked at his words. She stood dumbfounded as he continued to berate and insult her, stopping just short of calling her a whore.

There were sacred few things left I knew to be true beyond a shadow of doubt. One of those things was that Timbra Redfern was decidedly *not* a whore.

She was also *not* defending herself. She stood there, shoulders drooped in defeat, a million miles away from what was taking place right in front of her.

"Now wait just a minute, Mr. Redfern," I interrupted, knowing full well what was best and safest for me was to back away and let the two of them settle what seemed a family matter among, well, family. But Timbra had become *my* family, and I wasn't going to let the overbearing hulk of a man insult my friend, who I'd thought was meek by nature, but I was beginning to suspect was molded that way over time. "You're yelling at Timbra like she's been screwing the soccer team, and maybe you've been misinformed. That's not her." That was Bex, but I didn't want to get into *that*. "Timbra's a kind, intelligent, generous person with an exceptional moral compass. Accusing her of 'perverse escapades' is…well, it's hilarious, really, because she's the last person to be described that way."

"Is that so?" His eyes were squinted to angry slits; his voice gritty with menace. "So she's not sleeping with a dog? With that Adder boy?"

Words escaped *me* then. To confirm or deny Timbra's relationship with Boone wasn't my place. She was a grown woman and it was none of his business. On the other hand, I wanted to defend Timbra. Boone was wonderful for her, wonderful to her. They were crazy about each other, and very happy.

"It's true," Timbra squeaked from behind me, then cleared her throat and stated with more force, "It's true. I'm seeing Boone Adder. I like him very much, Father. I think I might love him."

Instead of espousing more rage at her admission, his face crumpled like sodden parchment. He turned his head, closed his eyes, and wheezed with suppressed emotion.

That was my cue to leave. I squeezed Timbra's hand to convey my solidarity and headed for Sabre Hall.

As I trudged up the wide stone steps, Pia alerted me to a note waiting at the front desk. *Oh hell*, I thought. *Gresham.* I snatched the note from my little mail slot behind the counter and opened the crisp white envelope with dread. But it wasn't from Gresham at all. I glanced ahead to the last line, which only held a scribbled "SD."

> *I'll be at the cafe on Ulmo Street today from 12:30 to 2:00.*
> *Would enjoy seeing you again.*
> *Dad and Granny say hello.*
> *SD*

SD, I thought. *Dad and Granny*? Then I got it. Stryde Drakontos. What the hell was he doing in town? During the day. And at a cafe, no less. I checked Pia for the time. It was 1:30 and I had another class at 2:00. I'd have to hurry.

16

Thankful for tracing in a time crunch, I went as far as I'd been downtown and used PiaMaps the rest of the way. Though it was mid-day, the street was so lined with old trees that it was shaded and cool. Several small tables lined the street ahead. It was impossible to be *too* cautious, so I peeked through the window of Cafe Bjorn. There were only a few patrons, but a booth at the back of the restaurant was conspicuously occupied. He wore a hat over his dark hair and sat low in the booth, but it was unmistakably Stryde.

Three little bells chimed as I entered, attracting the attention of a husky woman behind the bar. She nodded but never moved her concentration from the tasks behind the counter. Stryde saw me and started to rise, but I waved him back down and looked around nervously. The whole situation had me on edge.

I slid into the booth and wasted no time to whisper, "What are you doing here? Are you crazy?"

"No one will recognize me, Stella. I was young when I," he paused ever-so-slightly, "left, and I'm not so well known as Dad and Granny. Besides, I wore a disguise."

"The hat? Yeah, not fooling anyone. I knew you right away."

His lips turned up in what was meant to be a smile. It was the first time I'd seen him attempt one, to my recollection, and it was *off*. Like he'd borrowed it from someone and it didn't fit right. Maybe with some alterations or if he could fill it out better. In its current state, though, the gesture was disarming.

"Oh, here comes the waitress," I said. "She won't recognize you, will she?"

"Of course she will. I've known her since I was a child. Stella," he said as she approached, "this is Deandra Bjorn, an old friend of my family. Deandra, Stella—my cousin."

"It's true, then," she breathed. "You're Edina's. I didn't believe it."

I shrugged and mumbled "Nice to meet you" as she studied my features. She reminded me of the women I used to see back home—the ones you knew just by looking at them came from a long line of farming families. Strong-backed, barrel-chested women with biceps and quads that would put weight lifters to shame. Women who could give birth to a strapping son one day and be back on the tractor the next.

"So this is one of the people who's helping you?" I asked, once Deandra left for my water.

"Yes, Deandra's family and my family—your family—have been close for many years."

"How do you know that you can trust them?"

"Magical families like ours have always stuck together. We have to."

"What do you mean, 'magical families'?" I asked.

"Well, our family isn't your typically-evolved squirrel or salamander. We're descended of dragons, a mighty, magical creature. As is your father's omni blood," he mused. "So you have magical forbearers on both sides."

"Wait a minute. Are you saying 'magical creatures' like unicorns and merpeople? Is that what you're talking about?"

Stryde lifted a sleek black brow. "Merpeople are just regular people with aquatic ancestors. It's likely someone in your world caught a glimpse of one of us, and thus a myth was born."

"Uh-huh. And unicorns? You gonna tell me they're real, too?"

"Oh, don't be ridiculous," Stryde shook his head as if I'd lost my mind.

"*Me*? You think *I'm* being ridiculous?"

He didn't know how to respond to that. The implication of course was that's exactly what he thought.

"Deandra's family are great bears," Stryde went on after clearing his throat. "Besides their powerful natural animal forms, they're also magical skinchangers. They can inhabit the minds of animals. Or people. And because people fear being inhabited, throughout history Deandra's family has faced prejudice. Not to the extreme we dragons face now, but prejudice as a result of fear, nonetheless."

Stryde's green eyes clouded over as his thoughts took him far away. "Several hundred years ago a woman murdered her own husband, her entire family. When they caught her she claimed she'd been possessed. Fear spread like wildfire of the Bjorns and others like them. Everyone known to be a skinchanger was rounded up by mobs and accused of awful, evil things. People who the week before patronized the Bjorn's general store—who hired Deandra to babysit their children—they lost their minds to fear of the unknown, the unusual. They accused the neighbors they'd known their entire lives of intending to mind-rape them."

"My god. That's awful." I'd not heard the story, though it was similar to so many throughout history. Fear of the unknown, prejudice, and violence against those that were different. It was a tragic story that repeated itself time and again. "What happened? To the woman. To the Bjorns."

"The woman was discovered to be schizophrenic and had hurt her family in a psychotic episode. The Bjorns and others like them were innocent, though they faced continued prejudice. They do still, but refuse to back down. They opened this cafe. They continue to serve and help their neighbors in spite of everything."

"Exceptional people," I said.

"They are. They've been instrumental in our survival since escaping Brandubh."

I nodded and took another look at Deandra, this time with much more appreciation for her people, her history, her heart.

I came back to the present after a quick glance at the time. "Stryde, I'm sorry. I only had half an hour until my next class. I have to run. Is there something you wanted to talk about?"

"Oh," he said and blinked several times in short succession. "No." His disappointment was evident in his stiffened shoulders. "I only wanted to get to know you better."

The admission was a departure from the bizarre and detached demeanor I'd encountered before. "Oh, we've got plenty of time for that," I said and waved away his seriousness.

I left the cafe admiring Stryde's bravery for overcoming his crippling fear and myriad issues in order to get to know me, his estranged cousin, better.

17

Timbra never took the seat I saved her at our two o'clock Metamorphosis class. She didn't show for lab, either.

"Where's Timbra?" Boone asked. "It's not like her to miss class. I sent a text earlier, but she hasn't answered."

"Ah, her dad's in town," I evaded. Not my story to tell. "Last I saw, the two of them were talking outside Sabre."

"Oh. Okay," he said, but the wrinkle between his brow remained.

I really hoped Timbra and her dad could work through the issue. Boone was a great guy, and it was obvious that he and Timbra were crazy about each another.

They complimented one another like coffee and cream. Boone was funny and sarcastic without being insincere. He was personable in an almost forceful way—he made you like him, whether you intended to or not. Timbra, though, was an introvert and nearly froze with fear in social situations. She was as good as gold and had a whip-smart wit, but only a few close friends knew it. Boone and Timbra were one of those couples that were halves alone, but together made an exceptional whole. She tempered his outrageousness and he soothed her timidity.

Something was wrong. I knew it the moment I stepped foot in my room. I heard Timbra's sniffling, but I *felt* her despair. A fog of sadness so dense I nearly swiped the air around me permeated our adjoining suites. I tossed my books and Pia onto my chair and rushed through our shared bathroom before knocking on her door.

"Timbra? Can I come in?"

A hiccuped sob was the only answer. A hairline fracture started at the top corner and ran the length of my heart.

"Sweetie, I know you're there. And I know you're upset. Can I come in?"

I didn't wait for her answer, but pushed open the door. She lay face down in her bed, drowning in covers. All that was exposed were her tawny ears, and even those drooped. Her willowy form shook beneath the blankets as her body wracked with sobs.

My fractured heart cracked open completely upon witnessing the manifestation of her pain. Tears sprung to my own eyes, and I rushed to her side. I was at a loss what to do once I got there. All I could think to do was to lay my hand on her back. Maybe my presence was of some comfort.

After a while the shaking stopped, and so did her choked sobs. I sat motionless, afraid to breathe, and waited for her next move.

"Stella?" Timbra's voice was muffled beneath the blankets.

"Yes," I said just above a whisper.

"Will you get me a tissue? I'm covered in snot."

The statement caught me off guard and I chuckled in response. "Sure thing."

She extended one lithe hand from beneath the covers and I stuffed it with tissues.

A few moments later she emerged from her cocoon and sat up in bed. Her lovely face was a splotchy mess. She tried to rally, but was so downtrodden that her posture slumped, her eyes drooped in sorrow, and her lips threatened to quiver at any moment. She was on the verge of breaking down again.

"I never thought I'd say this, Timbra Redfern, but you look like hell."

She sniffed and wiped beneath her bloodshot eyes. When she found the nerve to swing them in my direction my breath left in a rush. Her eyes revealed such pain. I didn't have to ask to know that her father didn't change his mind about Boone.

"Wanna talk about it?"

She shook her head in an emphatic 'no.'

"Okay. Wanna get drunk?"

She nodded her head in an emphatic 'yes.'

"Perfect. I've got us covered."

I left to snag two wine glasses and a bottle of pinot noir from my little buffet. I turned to go back into her room, but heard a sharp intake of breath followed by a deep voice. The wine glasses were the least of my worries, and I started for her room when I realized who was talking.

"Timbra?" Boone pleaded, his voice pinched with concern. "My gods, Timbra, what's wrong? I've been trying to find you all afternoon."

She burst into tears again, and the bed creaked beneath Boone's weight as he rushed to her side. I returned the wine and glasses, and left my room to give the two some privacy.

It was dinner time, but I didn't much feel like dining alone. When I traced just outside Layla's door to invite her along I heard noises coming from her room, too. But these were on another plane than Timbra and Boone's emotionally charged situation. Moans and gasps seeped beneath the door, as did hushed words.

"*Wow. Okay,*" I thought. "*Guess Mari has the night off.*" I traced down to Sabre Bar, where I knew at least one friendly face would be.

Knox added clear alcohol to a tall glass, raising the bottle high while he poured in a dramatic flourish. He looked up and nodded when he saw me, mouthing "Hello Jeenjah," yet didn't spill a drop. I shook my head on a grin, and continued to watch as he snagged a long, thin cucumber slice and twisted it down into the glass.

"Hey, Stella," a woman's friendly voice rang from behind me. I squinted in confusion before comprehension dawned. Dread and disapproval weighed heavily in my stomach.

"Hi," I croaked before clearing my throat. "Hi, Mari. Looks busy tonight."

"Yes, for a Wednesday. You doin' okay? You look a bit pale."

"A long day," I evaded. Damn Layla. I adored Mari. I'd thought the two of them were happy together. Of course, I didn't know the details of their relationship. Maybe they weren't exclusive. *Best not to get into their business*, I thought. "See ya, Mari. I'm going to Cafe Row for a little dinner."

"All right, girl. Have a good one."

I closed my eyes and threw my head back at having one more thing to worry about. What a freakin' day.

I traced to the lovely collection of small restaurants that lined the cliff overlooking the Basel river as it meandered by the Radix campus. It had become one of my most treasured spots, and I relaxed a little as I approached my favorite purveyor of wood-fired pizza.

"Evening, Nick," I said and took a stool along the high bar that opened to the walk.

"Stella," he acknowledged. "The usual?"

My lips twisted despite my somber mood at the thought that I had a 'usual.' The small glass of wine he procured from thin air was heaven-sent.

"Your pizza will be right out."

I spun in my stool from the wood-fire oven to face the breathtaking view of the river and the fertile fields beyond. My neck held so much tension from the day—from the last several days—that it was tight and sore. I rolled my shoulders and stretched my neck from side to side, my eyes falling closed in reflex.

"I can help with that," a smooth male voice offered.

With my eyes still closed I took a deep breath and wished with every fiber of my being that it wasn't happening. But it was.

I peeked open an eye and found Rowan Gresham standing before me in all his masculine glory.

"Oh, god, help me," I said beneath my breath and scrubbed my eyes.

"No one can get you out of this conversation," he said with a smile that would melt a glacier. "Not even god."

"All right, Gresham," I said and steeled my nerves. "Let's do this."

He approached where I sat on the stool and sidled between my legs like he owned me. Warm hands gripped the back of my neck, and strong fingers massaged the base of my skull. He had such skill, such confidence, that it all happened before I remembered he was a lying bastard, I couldn't trust him, and we were through.

"No, Gresham," I whined. Then more firmly, "No. You wanna talk? Fine. But that's it."

He pulled his hands from my neck, making a point to run his fingers across my tender collar bone, but he remained between my legs. "It's not what you think, Stella," he said as he grasped the outside of my thighs, caging me between the counter and his body.

"Oh, that's a new one." It was obvious he had no intention of moving away from me. The pace of my heart picked up. I began to feel threatened. Frightened. I pushed hard at his stomach until he extricated himself from me, but he backed up only far enough that we weren't touching.

I sat up straighter and aimed for brave. "You've deceived me and withheld the truth at every opportunity. You say you care about me, but still you can't come clean—about things that directly involve me! I don't trust you for one second, Rowan Gresham, and this," I pointed between the two of us, "is over."

"Oh, it is *not* over, Stella," he growled and loomed over me. "I promise you that. I'll never let you go so easily. You think I got where I am by letting what I want escape my grasp?" He shook his head with a menace that made my blood run cold. "Think again." He'd stepped so close to me his hips pressed against my knees.

I had to look up at him, but I didn't back down.

"You don't want *me*, you arrogant asshole. You want to monitor and dissect me. To control me. And I strongly suspect you want to discover how you could use my rare forms to your advantage."

"Yes, Stella, your lineage is exceptional," he admitted. "Possibly unmatched in its potential. Do you think in my position as protector of Thayer I can let something like you just walk away? Something with the potential to protect or decimate entire populations? No. I will never do that. But rather than treat you like something to fear, I found you irresistible. Find you irresistible. I want you still, both for who you are and what you are."

He reached to caress my cheek but I flinched. *Something.* He'd said some*thing* rather than some*one*. He thought of me as a threat to be handled. A potential weapon like my mother's people. He wanted to harness me, and was using the oldest trick in the book to do it: seduction.

I was in a tight spot, out of which I couldn't see a clear path. My mind raced in search of options. If I ran now, Gresham would surely chase me. And he might realize there was no longer a way to catch me with honey. He'd go straight to vinegar, and although I hadn't yet seen that side of him, I had no doubt that Rowan Gresham could be bitter and foul. It was necessary I stay on his good side and find another way.

The beginnings of a plan began to form in the back of my mind. It was a long shot, and I wasn't sure how I'd do it, but it was a start; it was something.

"Stella, your pizza is read—" Nick cut off when he rounded the corner and comprehended the tension between Gresham and I. "Is everything all right, Stella?"

"Yes, Nick," I said and heaved a breath in relief. "Mr. Gresham was just leaving."

Gresham opened his mouth to protest, but when I said, "Can you take me to meet Gaspare Shaw tomorrow?" his body jerked with shock.

Rowan Gresham, always so in control, so put together, was at a loss for words. "Yes," he finally said.

"Great," I said with gusto. "I'll meet you at the Sabre lobby tomorrow at four."

He wasn't happy, but he accepted the deal. Gresham was nothing if not calculating, and he concluded it was the best offer he'd get. "I'll see you at four." He backed away from me, nodded at Nick, and then he was gone.

"Stella," Nick said as he fidgeted with the corner of his apron. "I try to mind my own business. But I've been around a long time. You'd best not get on that one's bad side."

I nodded distractedly. "I've learned that the hard way, Nick. I sure have."

I ate my pizza, but couldn't savor it. I was too preoccupied with the meeting I'd set.

I used Pia to look up information on Gaspare Shaw, and was pleased with what I learned. He was considered a fair leader. He'd held the post for years, and it looked as if he wouldn't face opposition any time soon. Thayer's prime minister was elected, and the qualifications were based not just on popularity, but also by the power one yielded.

While Thayer had no shortage of powerful magical beings, I could find no references to someone to compete with Shaw. As an omni, Gaspare Shaw had an inherent magical advantage. The ability to change into any animal trumped those with only one form. Besides being an omni he was known as gifted and knowledgeable in the art of magic.

I searched, but could find no references to a family. Perhaps a leader's personal life was off-limits in Thayer. That'd be a big change from what I'd always known.

I'd been gone for over an hour. *I should probably check in on Timbra*, I thought.

She was alone in her room and sat on the edge of her bed in a daze. When she heard me she looked up, and I couldn't contain my flinch at the haunted depth her eyes held. Her thin body sagged with desolation, loss.

"Oh, Timbra." I ran to her and clutched her to my chest. She devolved into sobs again, and I held her as she cried.

After a while she gave a loud sniffle and sat up. "Well, it's over. With Boone, I mean. I told him tonight."

"I'm so sorry," I said. And I was. "I guess your father wouldn't see your side of things?"

"No." She laughed, but it was devoid of joy. "No. He did not see my side of things. Said he'd pull me out of The Root if I didn't end it with Boone at once. And I don't want to leave, Stella. I'm meant to be here with you. With…our friends," she choked on a sob that found its way out despite her valiant attempt to suppress it.

"With Boone," I finished. "I know, sweetie."

"But my father's right," she sniffled. "We have no future. I know that. We could never have a family of our own. And my family would never accept him as my mate. I knew all of this from the start. That's why I fought getting involved with him. But," she hiccuped a sob. "I love him. Simple as that."

I blew out a breath at the unfairness of Timbra and Boone's situation. I wished I had a solution, but I couldn't see one.

"And Boone? Did he take it pretty hard?"

She could only nod, but then cleared her throat. "Angry," she whispered. "He's angry. Thinks I should've fought for us."

"But you did fight. It took a lot of guts to tell your father that you had feelings for Boone. I know your family is close, and it must've broken your dad's heart to see you making what he thinks is a huge mistake. And what more could you do, really? If he made you go back home you'd never see Boone anyway."

She shrugged and shook her head, as much at a loss for answers as I was.

"I'm sorry," I said again.

18

Timbra accompanied me to our three classes on Thursday, but her presence was limited to the physical. Her mind was somewhere else entirely. Boone didn't show at all. I, for one, was not looking forward to the first time the two encountered one another again. As close as our group of friends had become it was going to be tough. For a while.

"Hey," I said to Ewan as our Elements instructor passed an ancient stone amulet around the room.

"Hey." He didn't meet my eyes, but stared at his shoes.

"You heard then?" I asked.

"Yeah. We always meet for breakfast. When he didn't show I went to his room. Said he thought he'd just hole up for the day. Poor guy."

The reflexive twitching of Timbra's ears caught my attention. She'd heard us. Her face twisted with regret. Someone like Timbra couldn't turn off her feelings. Her broken face revealed she didn't want him to be sad and hurting any more than she wanted to feel that way herself.

Four o'clock rolled around much too soon.

I'd loosely formed a plan and the entire thing was dependent on Gaspare Shaw himself—someone I hadn't met and whose reactions and motivations I couldn't possibly predict. But it was the best shot I had at being released from Gresham's grasp.

As planned, I met Gresham in Sabre Hall's open common room. He was sleek and refined in black pants and a slim white button-down. My mind snagged on the memory of wearing nothing but a shirt just like it around his grand manor. I huffed a frustrated breath at myself, shook all thoughts of my romantic history with Gresham from my head, and approached him in a fantastic impression of nonchalance.

"Gresham," I said. "Shall we?"

His face was guarded, but confident, as he reached for my hand. I pulled it to my chest in reflex. I tried to recover and smile in a way that didn't come across frightened or disgusted or threatening, but I failed miserably.

Gresham closed his eyes and worked his jaw in irritation. "Have you been to Minister Shaw's office?" he grated.

I held my breath and shook my head. "Nope."

"How do you propose to get there, if you'll not let me touch you?"

"Good question," I said and sucked air through my teeth. "How about I touch you?"

His big hands fisted, but he nodded once in agreement.

I clasped onto his wrist, and before I could even secure my grip we were tracing through the frigid great nothing en route to my newfound uncle's government office.

"Brinda, please tell him we're here," Gresham grunted to the attractive middle-aged woman who was surrounded on three sides by large oak desks. She opened and closed her mouth like a fish out of water, but picked up the phone and did as she was bid.

I was nervous, and looked around the stately room in an effort to take my mind off of what—and who—awaited me.

Prime Minister Shaw's office antechamber wasn't opulent, but stark. The two small sofas on either side of his over-sized office door were adequate, functional. They weren't ornate or showy in any way. One or two plants broke up the hard lines of the waiting room; official pronouncements and recognitions lined the walls. But that was the extent of any decor.

From the corner of my eye I caught Gresham inspecting my every move. He'd gotten too close, was too intense. He was prepared to strike. I picked up a magazine from a nearby table and thumbed through it so as not to interact with him further.

Before I got through the cologne ads the tall wooden door between the sofas flew open and Gaspare Shaw emerged like a whirlwind. His searching gaze skipped right over Gresham and Brinda and honed in on me like a falcon to prey. He scrutinized my face with such intensity that I became uncomfortable and cast my eyes to the floor.

"Stella," he breathed and rushed to embrace me. It was so unexpected that I yelped and jumped out of his reach. I looked to Gresham, whose features were inscrutable. "I'm sorry," the man rumored to be my uncle said with conviction. "I forgot myself. Come into my office. Brin," he called over his shoulder, "coffee, please."

Once inside, my hands, my whole body, began to shake with nerves. I huffed and steeled myself, resolved to determine my own destiny. I walked toward a tall barrister where rows of well-loved books and an impressive collection of military commendations were displayed. A very early copy of *Don Quixote* held a featured spot atop a book stand. I dared not look at the publication date. Dared not touch it. Hell, as old as everyone in Thayer tended to be it was probably an original.

"Do you know de Cervantes?" he asked, his voice strained with hesitation...and hope. He was closer than I'd anticipated and I started again. I didn't yelp, though, and was proud of myself for that at least.

"No, I haven't met him," I said. "But I did read *Don Quixote*." I made a sideways smile in an attempt to lend my joke more humor. It didn't help. "I'm surprised to find it here. Why do you have it?"

"*Why*?" Gaspare's forehead creased with confusion. "It was the first modern novel, for one thing. But more than that, I've always thought Don Quixote an exemplary role model for leaders."

"The bumbling fool who put a pot on his head and challenged a herd of sheep," scoffed Gresham. "Be serious, Gaspare."

"I am serious, Rowan. But you're too frequently so." He turned to Gresham. "In fact, I find this disagreement a microcosm of the differences between you and I. Don Quixote may have been crazy, but he had conviction. Passion. He knew who he was. He had the courage not only to imagine the unconventional, but to pursue it. In seeking his passion he found joy, and even a sort of success. You, Rowan Gresham, are so blinded by the end game you fail to see joy along the way."

"Joy, madness—it's all the same," Gresham snarled.

"Stella. I'm sorry," said Gaspare, his eyes alight with kindness. "We're neglecting you. Rowan and I have been having this same argument in various forms for centuries. I fear we'll never agree. Let's talk about you instead. Rowan tells me you're adjusting exceptionally well at Radix, excelling in your coursework, and that you've developed an admirable control of your animal forms."

A scoff escaped my lips before I could stop it. "Did he? Did he actually say 'exceptional?' Because I don't think I've ever heard a compliment leave his mouth. I was led to believe that *I* was a bumbling fool."

Gaspare whipped his head in Gresham's direction before facing me again. "Mr. Gresham is not known for his tact, I'm afraid. He's a brilliant military mind, a fearsome fighter, a sharp investigator. But compassionate? Benevolent? Not so much."

"Yeah, I figured that out."

Gresham's heated stare could've melted an icecap.

"You have to understand I had no idea you were out there." Gaspare changed subjects, and intensity, with such speed that it took me a moment to catch up. "I was aware that Rowan was seeking out someone seen in a vision. As director of defense it's his job to know *everything* about *anything* suspicious…which skin morphing into shimmering scales definitely was, vision or no. But I never dreamed…" His deep blue eyes were lost beneath a fine sheen of clear liquid. *Tears.* He had teared up at the thought of finding me.

"Can you tell me about my father," I asked, my own throat thick with emotion. "I know very little. Only what I've heard from the legends, really."

Gaspare was silent for a moment, and I could tell memories of his brother filled his mind. He smiled wistfully and shook his head. "Gabrio was a bit of a dreamer. More so even than me. And an adventurer. Oh, the trouble he got into as a child," he laughed.

"The Shaw family has always been involved in the political scene because, as omnis, we are by nature some the most powerful creatures alive. But Gabrio wanted no part in the family's political interests. In fact he abhorred them, and after an argument with our late father, Gabrio left. We never heard from him again. We all thought he was living off the grid somewhere, but when centuries passed with no word, we feared the worst. I always held out hope he'd turn up one day with a bedraggled beard and a wild story."

He looked at me then with love in his eyes. Love, and loss.

"While I'm beyond thrilled to learn I have a niece, Stella, it's also a very sad time. If you're in fact descended of dragons, and the legend of Edina and the wolf is true…it means my beloved brother is dead."

After several tense moments he shook away his sadness and looked at an old watch. "Look at the time already. Stella, there's an appointment I cannot miss, but our conversation is far from over. Will you join me for dinner tonight?"

"I'd love that," I gushed.

"What time would you like us, Gaspare?" I glanced angrily up at Gresham's interference, and my irritation was noticeable even to Gaspare.

He looked from me to Gresham and back again. "I think it would be best if Stella and I spent some time alone, Rowan," Gaspare said. "We can get to know each other and catch up."

"Yes, but—" Gresham tried to say, but I cut him off.

"Sounds great. What time?"

I could hear Gresham teeth grinding to nubs.

"I'll send someone for you at eight," Gaspare replied with a smile.

"Perfect," I chirped and traced toward The Root—and away from a very irritated Rowan Gresham.

19

I had nothing to wear to Prime Minister Shaw's house, a fact I discovered approximately two and a half hours before I was expected. Timbra led me on a shopping expedition, a welcome distraction for both of us. With her help I purchased a flattering little black dress with clean, classic lines and a grown-up pair of heels. She fixed my hair and appointed me with jewelry from both of our collections.

When she let me see the result in the mirror the person looking back at me was…well, a woman.

"Oh, Timbra," I said turning from side to side. "Look what you've done. I'm all growed up."

Her laughter was like a wind chime—soft, melodic, and laced with fond memories."It's true," she said. "Look at your boobs—they finally came in."

I chuckled and turned to her. "You're sure you'll be all right without me? I hate to leave you. I can —"

"Hush. I'll be fine. A little heartache never killed anyone. Besides," her smile turned sad, "I'll still have it when you get back."

I hugged her from the side so as not to smudge or wrinkle, and whispered a sincere thanks.

At eight on the dot Pia alerted me to a visitor in the grand hall. I waved to Timbra and shot to the foot of the grand hall staircase.

Though Thayerians were used to the abrupt ins and outs necessitated by tracing, my presence nonetheless caught the attention of several in the hall.

One of those was Ewan, whose mouth fell open at the sight of me. He'd been talking to Pippa Tha Spinna, that gap-thighed spin instructor. She noticed the change in him and followed his gaze. When she saw me she jerked, surprise apparent in her pert, perfect features.

I turned more slowly than was necessary so they could all get an adequate look before setting my sights on my escort. He was young and gangly, though not unattractive, which I was thankful for since I'd apparently decided to put on a show.

"Ms. Stonewall," he said and bent at the waist. As he rose he extended a slender hand, and together we traced to my uncle's house, leaving my rapt audience behind.

"Oh, you have *got* to be kidding me," I said to my escort when we arrived at our destination. "Paul, tell me you're not serious with this house."

"Ma'am?"

"Is this really Mr. Shaw's house?"

"Yes. This is the traditional residence of the Prime Minister of Thayer. He also has a family home, of course. And a beach house. A cabin, too, though I've not been there."

I shook my head in awe. The place was gargantuan. And lovely. The grounds must have covered one-hundred acres. The gray stone residence featured a prominent entry, complete with towering statues flanking both sides of the limestone staircase.

As I slowly made my way up the stairs, I noticed the statues were carved into fearsome bears on the bottom and morphed into a big cat reminiscent of a leopard before forming a hawk who held in his beak a shiny metal ring. I turned my head to continue studying the statue after we'd passed. I hadn't seen anything like it. It wasn't totem-like in appearance, but rather a morphing of one animal to another.

And then realization dawned. It was an homage to omnis.

Paul lifted the hefty door knocker and let it fall one time. An austere man in a tuxedo opened the door and welcomed me in. Paul said goodbye, and indicated I was to follow the butler, whose posture was rigid, proper—except for his portly belly, which bounced jello-like with each footfall. He aimed for disinterested, but his eyes betrayed him. He raked my appearance from head to toe, monitored my every movement. I felt like I'd been administered a test—and failed.

The butler parked me in the "private study," and ordered I wait for Minister Shaw. Which I did. More books lined the walls of the room, as did gadgets and trinkets of varying origins. A globe sat in the middle of the room suspended by a polished wood rail. I went for a better look.

The landmass of Thayer was gigantic, the size of Eurasia. The rest of the globe was covered by the blue expanse of the ocean.

One of the primary features of the room, though, was a sixty-inch television opposite a brown leather sofa that called to my aching feet like a siren to sailors. I groaned inwardly at the inability to utilize it.

"Stella," Gaspare said warmly and entered from a door I hadn't noticed. "I'm so glad you came." He reached to hug me again, but thought better of it and instead clasped my upper arms. His smile was so genuine that my own face lit with pleasure.

"Thank you for having me," I said with formality.

Gaspare let go of my arms and backed away, noticing my dress as he moved. He took in my cocktail attire and then glanced at his own casual—though still bespoke—pants and woven shirt.

"I should have mentioned we would meet in a casual capacity. I'm sorry. I'm not used to this sort of thing."

"Oh, think nothing of it," I told him. "I wouldn't have chosen anything else for my first visit to the prime minister's residence."

He snorted without grace. "Please. I have to live here. I might as well be comfortable, and so should you. At least take your shoes off."

I declined *with* grace and accepted the cup of coffee he offered. Though his natural demeanor seemed to be genial and kind, the meeting was still awkward. We didn't know one another, had been brought together by loss, and the burden of the future sat heavy on our shoulders.

"You like baseball?" he asked.

"Baseba—yes," I stammered. "I do."

He turned on the big television with a remote from a nearby table before plopping down onto the sofa.

I wasn't sure what to do with myself. Gaspare Shaw was nothing like my expectations—hadn't been since the moment I met him. With few options left, I sat my coffee on a side table, took off my heels, and nestled into the corner of the sofa opposite him. He shot me an encouraging nod, and then became absorbed in the game.

"Pirates play the Cubs today," he said without looking at me. "Polanco is the best right fielder since Roberto Clemente. Don't you think?"

"Ah, sure." I shook my head in wonder. "You love baseball? American baseball?"

"Who doesn't?" He looked at me as if I had two heads. I let out a short laugh and we began a comfortable conversation about baseball. He knew a lot more than I did, particularly about historical teams and players, but that was because he'd been around for it.

"I was there for Clemente's walk-off inside-the-park grand slam in '56. He's still the only player to ever get one."

"You've been to my world, then?"

"Oh, many times. Thayer is my true love and my home but, well, we don't have baseball," he said as his sly grin crowded the corners of his eyes into a crinkle.

His features took on a more serious, reflective look. "Your father would have loved baseball, too."

"You think so?" My heart swelled as I imagined the man I never knew, beer in one hand and a hot dog in the other, stuffed into a stadium seat behind the plate. I was thankful for the new images; I'd been starving for details and memories just like this since I was old enough to remember.

"Do you have any pictures of him?" I dared ask. "I don't know what he looked like."

Gaspare made the slightest pause. "Ah, sure." He led me to the wall behind a stately desk. "Here's one of both of us at your age when we attended Radix." The two men stood side by side, each with an arm thrown around the other and toothy grins on their handsome faces.

"But," I stuttered. "He looks just like you." I shook my head. "The sandy hair, the olive skin, those eyes. Your nose. Everything. You two look just alike."

"You didn't know we were twins."

"No. I…I didn't."

"Yes," he said. "But he—your father—he was the best of us." Gaspare turned from the photo and lumbered back to the sofa, his body weary with the pain of loss. I followed him and took my seat.

"I'm sorry," I said. I lay my hand on top of his and squeezed. "For your loss. I'm sorry."

He cocked his head. "You're comforting me? It should be the other way around." He exhaled a heavy breath. "You're really something, Stella Stonewall." He squeezed my shoulder and pulled me into him in an awkward side hug. "Will you keep that name? Stonewall?"

"What? What do you mean?"

"Well, Stonewall is obviously a name your mother made up. Her name was Drakontos and your father's—mine—is Shaw. Will you take one of your parents' names or keep Stonewall?"

The thought had never entered my mind. I blew air from my inflated cheeks as I tried to form an answer. I couldn't come up with one, and shrugged.

He must have noticed my discomfort; he deftly changed the subject. "So, Rowan says you've made quite an impression at Radix…that you're an amazingly fast learner. 'Gifted' I think he said."

I made a noncommittal noise. "How do you know Gresham, anyway?"

Gaspare smiled and his face took on that sentimental, faraway look again. "We met at Radix. Rowan grew up in a tiny village on the east coast. He was a cocky bastard, changing from one form to another for audiences once he'd learned how. Gabrio and I thought to teach him a lesson. One afternoon he stood on the lawn outside Sabre Hall putting on a show. Oh, the girls loved it. Loved him; they always have. He thought he was so special."

Gaspare laughed, his gaze lost in the distance as he recollected his youth. "Gabrio and I knew just what to do. We were so close, so in sync, it only took one look. When Rowan shot to the sky as a bird, we took the same form and chased him. He couldn't escape two of us and changed into a big raptor. We did, too. I remember so clearly the look in his eyes the moment he realized what he was up against. He dove for the ground and rolled into a growling bear. Gabrio and I landed on each side of him, exploded into tigers, and leapt at him."

Gaspare shook his head and lifted one side of his mouth. "It was the first time I'd ever seen Rowan laugh. He's always been so serious. When he knew he was beat he stood on two feet and laughed with such joy. Afterward, he put an arm around us both and said, 'How about I buy you boys lunch?' We were inseparable for years after."

"Inseparable," I interrupted. "You, my father—and Gresham?"

"Yes. Well, until our father died. He—your grandfather—had always thought Gabrio would make a better leader than I. As our father lay dying he pressured Gabrio to vie for the position. Begged him to promise he'd do it. But Gabrio'd never had any interest in leading Thayer, had made it clear for years.

And that's when he disappeared. I lost my father and my brother. It was a very hard time for me."

"I'm so sorry," I said.

Gaspare looked up with a start. "Oh, look at me! Having a pity party over wounds long healed." The depth of sadness in his eyes held rivaled my own. "You and I, we're no strangers to loss, are we?"

"No, unfortunately not. But I'm so glad to have found you. For a lot of reasons."

"We're family now," he said.

I reached to squeeze his hand, but he pulled me toward him in a tight hug. It was odd at first, but I soon closed my eyes and relaxed into the embrace. I was completely blissed out from finding him, liking him, and from his open acceptance of me. I relished the tender moment for as long as I could.

But my visit had a purpose besides getting to know Gaspare Shaw and learning about my father. I had other, more immediate and self-preserving needs.

"It feels weird to know Gresham and my father were such close friends," I said once I'd righted myself on the sofa.

"Weird? Why?" The curious turn of his head was almost parrot-like.

"Well, I know age is a more pliable thing here in Thayer than where I grew up, since you all live longer, but," I bit my lip and held my eyes wide, "dating someone who was childhood friends with my father has a certain 'ick' factor, don't you think?"

Gaspare went completely still. I don't think he breathed for several long moments. His face betrayed nothing as he stared straight ahead at the baseball game. But I could sense rage forming around me. Rage…and power.

Oh, he was pissed all right. I had hoped he'd feel protective of me, and our short time together had provided for a bond—for me, too—stronger than I'd dared anticipate. If anyone could get Gresham off my ass without endangering me further, it was his longtime friend and boss—the leader of the land and people he was sworn to protect.

"Are you interested in dating Gresham," Gaspare asked without inflection. He was being so careful.

"No, not really," I said with a diffidence I didn't feel. "But he's pursued me pretty hard, and you're right—he does have a way with the ladies."

The flare of a nostril was the only indication of his internal boil. "I'll take care of it," he said stiffly.

I preened, pleased with the success of both my plan and my performance.

Dinner was served while we finished the baseball game in the private study. Despite the presidential surroundings and our fledgling relationship, the evening was so casual, so…normal.

Gaspare was more than I'd ever hoped to find when I learned about my father, whom we talked about for nearly two hours.

I covered my mouth as I yawned, my legs curled under me on the sofa. Someone had started a fire and I was warm and happy. *And loved.* I felt loved.

"It's late. You have school tomorrow," Gaspare said and then chuckled. "Don't worry. I know you're not a child. And it looks like you've done a hell-of-a job on your own."

"Thanks," I said and stood.

"We've got all the time in the world to get to know one another," he said. "But a lot to catch up on. I'll send your Pia my information. Let's get together this week?"

I left the mansion lighter than I'd felt in a very long time.

When I arrived back at Sabre there was a small, delicately wrapped present for me in my mail slot.

"Who left this?" I asked the desk clerk.

"Courier brought it."

I took the gift to my room and pulled open the gauzy ribbon. Beneath the crisp white wrapping paper was a box of four decadent chocolate truffles. No note.

Ohhhh, Gresham, I thought. *Bad timing. You don't know what's hit you yet.*

But it would have been wasteful not to enjoy the smooth, rich chocolate infused with orange and ginger, and I have always been very conservation-conscious.

20

What Timbra needed was a night or two away from The Root. Away from the ever-present risk of running into Boone and any resulting heartache and awkwardness. Break-ups were difficult—at least this one was.

I'd found a brochure for an eclectic bed and breakfast up north when I stopped for my now-annihilated box of truffles. The cabin boasted a pool and small spa, and specialized in rejuvenation. It seemed fated.

In Thayer, instead of taxis, an escort system is used. Since tracing is painless, quick, and free, Timbra and I could literally go anywhere on the extensive landmass in a matter of seconds. The only problem, of course, was getting somewhere we'd never been. That's where escorts come in.

I spoke to a woman by phone who agreed to meet Timbra and I at the exterior gates of Radix. She would lead us to the cabin for our relaxing weekend. Simple.

"That must be her," Timbra said, her eyes bright with excitement. She was thrumming with happiness to get out of town, to have a distraction. The swelling around her eyes from crying since her break-up with Boone on Wednesday had all but disappeared.

It was a relief to find something to help Timbra besides commiserate…and hand her tissues. The prospect of our weekend had perked her up quite a bit.

I was excited for selfish reasons, too. Having been fairly confined to The Root, I hadn't seen much of Thayer. Each new adventure felt like opening another bedroom door of my new home.

"Loryn?" I called to the woman just beyond the gate. She turned, and when our eyes met her wide mouth opened to expose a blinding number of perfect white teeth.

"Stella, hello," she said. "You two are going to have a great weekend. Any questions before we set off?"

We had none, and threw overnight bags over our shoulders before forming a circle to hold hands with Loryn. One brief, cold shot of darkness later we stood before the most impressive log cabin I'd ever seen. But calling it a "cabin" made little sense. A mansion made from logs better described it.

"Let me take those bags, ladies," Loryn said. We were both so awe-struck that she slipped them from our shoulders without argument.

Double front doors were flanked first by large plate-glass windows and then farther out by…trees. Two enormous trees with gnarled roots as tall as I was formed the pillared base of the front porch. The trunks were sanded and polished until they shined, and they extended all the way up to support the roof of a third story.

Nearly the entire facade of the house was made of glass. I spun around to see what view these windows had been installed to reveal, and my breath left on a dreamy, pleased sigh.

"Oh, it's so beautiful, Loryn," Timbra gushed. "I can't believe we get to stay here."

Me either, I thought, but was still too enthralled to speak.

Only a small copse of pointed evergreens let on that the snow-capped mountains in front of us did not, in fact, extend up *and* down. The lake's waters were so still and clear that the reflection of the blue sky and breathtaking mountain range was nearly impossible to distinguish from the original.

I shook my head in wonder and whispered, "Just gorgeous."

"You're welcome to explore the lake, the base of the mountain, and the forest surrounding the property. Or, you can relax poolside all day between massages and facials—your call, ladies," she said and flashed another big smile. Her dark curls bounced merrily as she led us into the "cabin."

"Is this your home," I asked her. "Or are the B&B and spa business ventures?" Everything was so lovingly done, so homey, that it didn't feel like a business.

"This is our family home, actually. After my siblings and I all left my father considered selling. He was lonely, and it's far too much house for one person. My husband and I were in the hospitality industry and made the choice to come home and keep the place in the family. We couldn't bear the thought of losing it. We've only been open a month, but have most of the kinks worked out."

"This place is amazing," I said.

"Thank you. I hope you feel as at home as we do while you're here." Loryn led us up a spiral staircase built of carved and polished wood. It blended into the rest of the house, which was serene, tasteful. "Your room, ladies." She opened the door to reveal a bedroom with two double beds and an adorable sitting room. The French doors to the balcony stood open and a crisp breeze brought with it the scent of juniper.

"I have died and gone to heaven," I said, and threw myself onto a cushioned chair. The mountain air filled my lungs, and replaced most of my worries with cleansing thoughts of the endless tiny joys of nature. It was as if the evergreens had invaded my senses and were using their redolent foliage to scrub away the fear, the uncertainty, the betrayal, and loss. My eyes remained closed as I welcomed the relaxing atmosphere deep into my pores.

Loryn was speaking. "If you need anything I'll be just downstairs. Breakfast is at nine. Your massages are scheduled for ten-thirty. Make yourself at home with the pool in the back, or any of our amenities."

"Thank you, Loryn," Timbra said. "I can't tell you how much I need this weekend."

Loryn smiled warmly, her dark eyes glistening with kindness in the overhead light. "Oh. I nearly forgot. We do have other guests, along with my little brother and his friend, for the weekend. This place is big enough to house a small army, though, so you should still feel like you have plenty of privacy."

We showed her out and thanked her again.

I hung my clothes in the closet and turned to Timbra with a wicked grin. "Pool?"

"Pool," she nodded.

"These people either are wolves or are freakishly obsessed with them," Timbra said as we made our way through the open expanse of the main house.

"What makes you say that?"

"Did you see those doors when we first arrived? Wolves carved into them. Snarling wolves. Not exactly a hospitable relief for someone of cervid decent, eh?"

"Ohhh. I didn't even notice. Yikes. You okay to stay?"

"Sure, sure," she assured me. "Just a lot of wolf-y stuff around for a B&B."

We were beyond pleased to find an outdoor kitchen and bar area with a chalk sign indicating we should help ourselves and keep track of any beverages consumed.

"Would you look at that," I said. "The honor system. How quaint."

"You're far too jaded for someone our age."

"I don't think I'm jaded," I said as my bottom lip found its way atop the other. "Sarcastic, maybe."

She grunted, but said nothing further.

"I'm going for a beer. Want anything?" I asked.

"My gods, yes. Not much beats a cold beer poolside on a hot day, does it?"

We sat in contented silence enjoying the warming embrace of the sun, the cool relief of our drinks, and the magical worlds of our books.

I was almost asleep on my chaise when I felt Timbra's concentrated gaze. "So, your mom's a fabled murdering dragon who tortured and killed helpless Thayerian people. And you, my friend, turn scaly, too."

Hell. I had hoped that her troubles with her dad and Boone would cause her to forget about me for a while. My particular problems certainly hadn't been foremost on her mind the last few days. But it was imminent the dreaded conversation be had at some point. And the time had arrived.

I swallowed, but found no relief for my dry mouth. "Yes," was all I could say.

"Are you worried you'll lose yourself in a vicious rampage? Is there a risk of that? Tell me honestly. I'll still love you, and I'll find a way to get you help if you need it."

"I know you would," I croaked before clearing my throat. "And I can't tell you how much that means to me. You're my bosom good friend, Timbra Redfern. I promise to never set you aflame with my dragon fire."

"This is serious, Stella," she admonished.

"I know it's serious. Trust me. I've been a knot of nerves and disgust and shame since I learned who and what I am. It's why my mother really left me, in case you hadn't pieced that together. She couldn't face telling me. It's why she left Thayer so many years ago, why she raised me alone, why she didn't tell me about my father."

Timbra didn't say anything. Didn't look at me. She took a sip of her beer and stared past the pool.

I took a solidifying breath and went on, "Add to that steaming heap of bullshit the fact I learned the only reason Gresham pursued me was to control me, to acquire me as a weapon himself…well," I took a swig of my own beer. "Not a whole lot left to build a great self image. It's serious, all right. Seriously screwed up. *I* am seriously screwed up."

"Oh, Stell," she said, and scooted to sit at the end of my chaise. Her doe-like eyes held such compassion, such love that

I struggled not to break down. "I didn't know about Gresham. And I'm sorry that you've been keeping this secret for so long. That must've been excruciating. I wish you'd trusted me."

"I do trust you! I do. But my god, Timbra. The significance of this whole thing. The stigma it carries with it. People hate dragons. They think we're Satan's spawn, and for good reason. If word got out about me—are Thayerians known for burning people at the stake? 'Cause that's what I envision. And Gresham and Professor Lochlain advised me to guard the secret with my life, too."

"I won't tell a soul," she said, then more soberly, "I know there's not an evil drop of blood in you. This changes nothing as far as I'm concerned."

"I don't deserve you, Timbra." Tears spilled over my eyelids. I swiped at them to remove the evidence.

"No you don't," she said with a kind smile. "But we've got plenty of time for you to work on that."

"I think I'd like my sun hat. I left it upstairs. Need anything?"

Timbra had gotten very quiet. Whether she was thinking about me or Boone, I didn't know. She shook her head but didn't answer.

My gauzy cover whipped in the light mountain breeze as I entered the back door of the house. *Damn. Forgot the key.* I changed course for the front of the house, where a small enclave housed the B&B office. When I poked my head in I saw that Loryn wasn't alone. A man stood in front of her desk in swim trunks. The wide expanse of his back was bronze, and tapered down to perfection. *Loving the views here*, I thought, and couldn't stop my goofy grin before Loryn caught my eye.

"Come on in," she said with a wave. "Stella, this is my brother."

My heart came to a screeching halt in my chest before resuming with thunderous force. I stood stunned for several beats until comprehension dawned. My head back fell back as I laughed. Of course he was her brother. *Of course.* I laughed because I knew the stars were surely laughing, too.

Ewan wasn't sure what to make of my hilarity, but he stood with a good-natured grin while I finished. "Whatcha doin here?" He looked at home in the log mansion in the mountains. Only natural. It *was* his home.

"Timbra and I are getting out of town for a girls' weekend, getting away from—" The joy bled from my face. "You're not here with Boone are you?"

"Yes, we're headed to the pool. I left before he did so I could stop and see my sis— Stella? Where are you going?"

I ran for the pool, intent on thwarting Boone and Timbra's undesirable reconciliation.

"It's okay," Ewan said as he caught up to me. "We've got a few minutes. He's still upstairs."

"Shit, shit, shit," I said. "This is just awful, Ewan. What am I going to say to her?"

I ran over scenarios in my head. All of them ended badly: with Boone and Timbra meeting by chance and ruining the entire weekend.

Yet despite the risk we faced my heart was full, giddy even, and delighted in my circumstances. The traitorous thing was happy to see Ewan.

"Don't worry about it," he said and closed the space between us. "I'll come up with a reason Boone and I must leave. We won't ruin your stay."

"No." I shook my head. "We'll go. I'm not running you out of your own home. I'll fake sick or something."

"Stella," Ewan said, his tone serious, determined. "I want you to be here—to love it here. There's no way I'll let you leave."

"Well," I said, uncomfortable with the sudden weight his words had taken on. "We're at an impasse."

"It would seem so." He thought for a moment, his impossibly deep brown eyes lost in concentration. "Tell you what. I'll keep Boone busy in town this afternoon, then come up with a reason we have to leave tonight. It'll be fine. There's a soccer game at The Root we wanted to catch tomorrow, anyway."

"She'll be devastated if this doesn't work. She can't face him right now."

"It'll work," he said. "It's just a few more hours."

"Are you sure? I don't want to leave, it's true. This place is…it's glorious, Ewan. You said you grew up in a cabin in the woods," I accused. "This is hardly a cabin."

His cheeks pinked in embarrassment and his gaze shot to the floor. "This was my parents' dream," he said just above a whisper. "They were happy here. We were all happy here." He cleared his throat. "I'd better get to Boone if we're going to make this work."

I nodded my agreement.

He raised his gaze to mine and squeezed my hand. "This will all work out. They just need more time."

To further reduce the risk of running into the boys I drug Timbra out of the house to explore the lake. She was a swift-footed hiker—no surprise there. We enjoyed a snack of local cheeses and fresh bread near the water, and lay atop a patch of soft green moss. We passed the time in peace, gazing at the clouds.

"What do you wanna do tonight?" I ran the fine silt I'd discovered along the edge of our mossy perch through my fingers.

She answered right away. "I really think we should go out."

"Out? Like, to a club?"

"Dancing. Definitely. I want to have a couple drinks and just *forget* on the dance floor for a little while. Surely there's someplace not too far from here."

"Out," I shrugged. "Okay then. I'll ask Loryn. See what she recommends."

Timbra bit her bottom lip and grinned at the prospect of a little fun. As she stood I thought I saw the tilt of her ears perk up the tiniest fraction. "Time for our facials," she said. "Better head back."

21

Loryn recommended a place in town that hosted local musicians on Saturday nights. Ewan assured me he and Boone would be long gone by then, and that we could have all the fun we could stand without fear of bumping into them.

It was clear an hour and a half into the night what Timbra's intention was: obliteration. I didn't blame her, really. She'd been nursing a dreadful heartache. And I knew as well as anyone the driving desire to be rid of the oppression of loss and sadness. One night of overindulgence wouldn't hurt anything.

The band was surprisingly good, and when they played an upbeat song Timbra yanked me up by the arm. She threw her head back and her arms out wildly. "Let's dance!" she said.

I indulged her. I had nothing against fun, after all. Timbra's lithe body swayed and rocked to the beat, assisted by some fairly potent margaritas. Without fail, the occasion of two girls dancing together served as some unspoken invitation for horny strangers to jump on back. I shook my head sharply and shooed them away.

Timbra, though, was less forceful.

"Hey," I warned a lanky guy whose hips seemed to move on hinges, "Were your parents octopi or something? Keep your hands to yourself!"

He smirked, mitigating any handsome that might have been found in his face. "She's not complaining," he said and popped Timbra soundly on the ass. "You're the only one here with a problem." He turned from me, dismissing me well before I was through.

"Listen, asshole," I yelled to be heard above the music. "She's had too much to drink to realize what you're up to. But *I* haven't. You and her," I flicked my finger back and forth between them. "Not happening. She's in love with someone else."

"I'm not looking for *love*, darlin', just a little *lovin'*." He was behind Timbra, and banded one arm above her chest, the other at her hips, and pulled her tightly into his body. He stuck his nose to her hair and inhaled before lowering his mouth to the back of her neck. He stared at me with vengeful eyes as he pressed his lewd lips to her, daring me to do something about it.

I was steaming mad. At him. At his audacity. And furious with Timbra for getting herself into the situation. My hand was on its way to snatch her from his grubby tentacles when I heard a growl from the door so low and menacing it made the hair on my arms stand up. The warning was audible even over the music, and every eye in the place shot to the door.

When I saw what stood at the bar's entrance I gasped and involuntarily stepped away, though the beast was nowhere near me.

A vicious dog the size of a sofa stood nearly to the shoulders of the people at the bar. Even in the low light I could see that its golden hair was ruffled at the neck, a clear indicator of its intent to attack. Those closest to the beast scrambled away, clearing a better line of sight. Some crazy person approached the maddened dog, and I shook my head back and forth, silently willing him not to go near it.

Surprise suffused my spine like I'd suffered an electric shock. The man approaching the beast was Ewan—which meant...the beast was Boone.

"Oh, hell," I breathed. "Oh, no."

The dog stalked toward us, his rumbled growls growing more ferocious with every pace of his heavy paws. When Octoman finally realized he was the one in the dog's sights, he threw his arms away from Timbra so dramatically it was almost comical. Almost. The palpable pull of imminent danger sucked any humor from the space.

Boone's wide snarl revealed pointed teeth the size of small daggers. My every instinct told me to run. Instead, I grabbed Timbra by the bicep and threw her behind me. I'd never been around Boone's animal form and he looked violent as hell. I feared Timbra might bear the brunt of his fury. But he was intent on Octoman.

Mangled words escaped Boone's slathering mouth. "Hands. Off. My. Woman."

The dancing idiot had the nerve to smirk again. To taunt the angry beast. "She wasn't complaining."

Boone roared with fury, deafening those of us closest to him. It scared me. I admit it. I backed away and took Timbra with me.

Timbra, who at that point decided to clue in to her surroundings.

"Boone Adder," she admonished. "Stop barking, for gods' sake. This is none of your concern."

His eyes widened with outrage before he uttered a nearly imperceptible, "You. Next."

Ewan had positioned himself between Boone and Octoman. Not his most brilliant move, in my opinion.

"Let's go, darlin'," Octoman said before running his arm around Timbra's shoulders.

I shook my head in disgust. I knew what came next. The guy was an obstinate fool. *He might just deserve an ass whooping*, I thought.

With a powerful thrust from his back legs, Boone launched himself toward the guy, knocking Ewan to the side.

Boone had Timbra's suitor pinned for three seconds, snarling wetly in his face before Octoman changed—not into an octopus, as I'd imagined—but into some sort of half-crocodile, half-human combination. He used a thick armored tail to knock Boone off of his body, then bolted upright on stumpy legs.

His face, which had looked so natural in a snarl, elongated to house a fearsome row of jagged teeth. He snapped them with force, and the crowd erupted in a mass exodus from the bar. Timbra watched in awe as the two predators circled each other. Searching for a weakness. Readying to attack. I looked to Ewan to see what we could do, but he shook his head at me in a direct warning to steer clear. I was on board with that program. Getting between those two seemed a good way to lose a limb.

The snarling, grunting sounds of a fight brought my attention back to Boone and his adversary. Boone had launched himself again, breaking a pub table and one chair as they fell to the floor. They rolled on the grimy dance floor, biting and clawing at one another. Boone tried repeatedly to tear the man's skin, but he had none. Tough armor protected him. Frustrated and enraged, but still with his wits about him, Boone faked for the croc's neck. When he dodged to protect the area, Boone's wide mouth clamped down on the croc's reptilian eyes.

"Boone, stop!" Ewan roared and rushed toward them. He skidded onto his knees and followed Boone's movements until he caught his wild gaze. "Boone, listen to me. You can't kill this asshole. I know you want to, but you can't."

The beast's big body heaved with infuriated breaths. His canines bit into the croc's head like an evil vice and one eye began to bleed.

"Boone," Ewan said, "Let him go. You've won. He'll not touch Timbra again."

"*Gumph*," the croc grunted to the best of his ability.

Boone took the sound for argument and shook the poor man's head like a chew toy. I heard more muffled sounds, though these were pained and hopeless, before the croc's body went limp.

"Let him go, Boone," Ewan pleaded once more.

The great dog widened his mouth and the croc's scaled and bloody head dropped to the floor with a thunk.

Timbra had begun to weep silently behind me, and when she saw the man's still body she whimpered, "Is—is he dead?"

"No," Ewan said as he rose from the body. "But he's lucky he's not. Dumbass." Then he looked to Boone. "Both of you. Dumb." Boone snarled at Ewan, but without conviction.

I looked around the mangled bar. The fight had resulted in several broken chairs and at least two flattened tables. Glass shards scattered the floor.

"I'll make it right," Ewan told a leather-skinned man behind the bar. "Send notice to my dad's house and I'll take care of it." The man scowled, nodded once, and turned away.

"What now?" I asked.

"Now," Ewan said, "We go home. If you can manage Timbra, I'll handle Boone."

I held my head in my hands, trying in vain to be patient with Timbra. She'd been crying since we returned to our room at the B&B. She was a sniveling, self-deprecating wreck. I didn't try too hard to make her feel better about the situation because it was, in at least some small way, her fault.

Her ears twitched seconds before a knock sounded on our door. She dried her tears with a newfound exuberance, and I suspected her sensitive ears had detected Boone outside. My suspicions were confirmed when I heard a muffled, "Timbra? I'm so sorry. Please open the door."

I looked to Timbra, whose bottom lip quivered at the sound of his voice.

"You want me to send him away?"

"No," she said. Then more firmly, "No. We need to work through this. Can you give us some privacy?"

I opened my mouth to protest, but she stopped me. "It'll be fine. Really."

"If I were you, I'd try to keep things cool," I said with a dubious look. "Remember who'd win in a dog-on-deer fight." She rolled her eyes. "I'll take Pia. Just call if you need me."

She agreed and I traced to the mossy area along the lake we'd explored earlier in the day.

I have always liked being alone. It's the only time I ever truly relax. No pressure to be interesting, no worries about pleasing someone or protecting feelings. Being alone *and* outdoors was the epitome of perfection. Just me and nature. I lay back on the moss, breathed deeply of the evergreen air, and lost myself in the night sky.

Far removed from the bustling city, where light pollution was nonexistent, I could see a thousand stars. Before coming to Thayer I had studied astronomy. My coursework lent me a substantial knowledge of stars, galaxies, and their physics. But science couldn't explain the wonder, the joy, the peace that inflated my heart whenever I studied the glorious night sky.

I read once that eighty percent of people in my world had never seen the Milky Way—couldn't see it because of over-illumination. Streetlights, billboards, and the like allow light to spill outward, reflecting off moisture and dust in the air to create a glow that obscured the stars—light pollution.

But somewhere along the line Thayerians had designed lights that focused illumination downward. *One more reason to love my new world*, I thought, as I lay on my little knoll with an uninhibited view of the galaxies.

I was happy. Relaxed. And no longer alone.

"I see you got your dog back on its leash," I teased.

"I had to chase him down. And he bit the hell out of me. But I did it."

I turned my head to the side to find Ewan standing beside me. He smiled down at me, his chocolate curls falling loosely around his face.

"Mind if I join you?"

"Not at all." I was surprised at the depth of the truth in my statement. Despite the desire to be alone, I wanted Ewan Bristol's companionship more. He lay down on his back beside me on the soft moss in companionable silence for several moments. I listened to the pleasant sound of his breathing, relished the warmth supplied by the proximity of his body.

Eventually I said, "Why did you come to the bar? You said you'd occupy him elsewhere."

He grunted. "We were leaving the cabin after saying goodbye to my sister when the strangest look flew across Boone's face. He darted around the room like…well, like a dog who'd picked up a scent. He knew Timbra'd been in the house."

"Oh shit," I gasped.

"Yep. He tracked her right up to your room. He banged so long and so loud on the door that I finally had to come clean. When I did, he insisted on joining you guys—that he could control himself, would make an effort to be friendly. I was stupid to agree to it."

"You can say that again."

"Hey," he objected, but it held no bite. "We'd just walked in the door when he saw that asshole's hands all over Timbra. He lost it. One minute he was struck dumb with pain and the next he morphed into his dog—a very pissed-off version of his dog."

"Damn, he was scary," I said. "He's so playful and aloof I imagined a bounding goldendoodle or something. Nu-uh. More like a giant zombie pitdoodle." I shuddered at the memory.

"Apparently the ancient Molossians were like mastiffs…but bigger. They guarded homes, flocks. Not something you'd want to run into on a dark night," he said.

"Nope."

"What got into Timbra?" he asked. "What the hell was she thinking?"

"Tequila—that's what got into her."

"Ah," he said, as if it explained everything. "What do you think the two of them are up to now?"

"In their states of mind? Fuckin' or fightin,' one of the two. Though…maybe both."

Ewan barked a laugh. "I love your accent," he said.

"You're the one with an accent," I laughed. He had moved closer to me while I spoke. When I looked up, his face was a whisper away from mine. "I don't think this is a good idea, Ewan." I said the words but didn't—couldn't—move my face from his.

"Oh, I think it's a very good idea," he said and rubbed his nose along mine.

"But," I sputtered. "I'm just coming off this thing with Gresham."

Ewan stilled, and I swear I heard a rumble deep in his chest. A rough exhale sent his hot breath across my cheek. My own breath was stuck in my throat. Much too soon Ewan began rubbing his cheek against mine, moving his nose along the sensitive skin under my chin. Goosebumps erupted along my neck and shoulders.

"And I need…to…figure things out…before I…get involved…with someone." I was having difficulty concentrating.

"I think kissing would be all right, don't you?" he asked, his breath hot against my ear.

"No…I mean…I guess kissing wouldn't hurt anything," I said, my backbone dissolving into the moss beneath it.

Ewan was on my mouth before the last word escaped it. His hair brushed my cheeks as he pressed his soft lips to mine. A sweet, chaste kiss. I closed my eyes, delighting in the simple pleasure of his skin on mine.

There have been a number of iconic kisses throughout history. Goodbye kisses, kisses of possession, tragically lost and then reunited kisses. My theory is that most of these took place when the threat—or promise—of sex was removed from the equation. Without sex as a consideration, all thought, all effort, all the force of one's need goes into the kiss itself. It becomes performance art—something to be enjoyed both in the moment and later, when the tiny intricacies and nuances of the kiss can be replayed over and over.

This kiss was art. Ewan and I became so in tune with one another that our passion played on a loop. We kissed, learning what one another preferred. As our understanding of the other's needs increased, so too did pleasure, which led to more—and more intense—kissing.

There were no seeking hands, and our clothes remained intact. It was the most perfect kiss, more so than I could have even imagined. When the force of it left me without breath, the kiss broke, and with it the spell we were under.

"Goodnight, Stella," Ewan said. He pressed his swollen lips to mine once more, and then he was gone.

22

"Stella, the location of your Monday/Thursday metamorphosis advisor meetings have changed," Pia intoned bright and early on Monday morning.

"Oh?" I said and slipped on my favorite jeans. "To where? Who changed them?"

"The location is now the residence of Prime Minister Gaspare Shaw. You're really moving up in the world."

I moved closer to her so that she could see me roll my eyes. "Who changed the meetings, Pia?"

"I received a request from the prime minister's secretary, Brinda. I took the liberty of confirming for you."

"What makes you think that's a change I'd want to make, Pia?"

"I'm inanimate, Stella, not stupid. When the PM says trace, you ask where to." I barked a laugh. "Stella," she said, her tone leading.

"Hmmm?"

"Why have you been ignoring me? You're not confiding in me anymore. Your student journal entries are almost nonexistent. I feel we've grown apart."

I rubbed my eyes with the heels of my hands. How to tell your personal interactive device that you fear she's a surveillance tool for those who'd do you harm? "I'm just busy, that's all, Pia."

"I'm not reading too much into this neglect. I know what's going on. Have you found a newer model? Is it that TwitBit? I heard she'll give you a nasty rash."

"Stella," grated a voice laced with fury. *Ugh. Gresham.*

My eyes squeezed closed as I willed him to just go away. But I could never get that lucky. I was going to have to deal with this, with him. We needed to find some closure so we could both move on. I stretched my neck to each side in an effort to release the tension I suddenly felt before turning to my former lover.

"Gresham," I said, pasting a grin on my face. "How ya been?"

His chest expanded on a breath I knew he took to avoid throttling at me. "Where were you this weekend?"

"That's none of your business." I took a bite of salad, making sure to stab a piece of lettuce, a cranberry, and an almond. *Whoops. Forgot the feta cheese.* I concentrated on my fork, my food.

Gresham's lips flattened in irritation and the veins on his arms inflated as his fists clenched at his sides. "You can't be careful enough. If anyone discovers what you are you'll not make it through this. We still need to work on a plan."

"Oh, I remember your plan," I said and sat back in my chair. "You want me to capture my own family, to help sentence them to death."

"Your family?" He arched a black brow. "Since when are you so chummy? Since when do you care?"

"Ah. I don't. We're not." I tried to recover. Tried not get flustered and reveal more than I intended.

"Well they sure as hell didn't hesitate to betray you," he said low in his throat.

"I know that. You think I don't know that? But I'm not going to hunt them down, Gresham. Two wrongs don't make a right. I can't do it. I won't. I'll find another way."

"There is no other way. They're killers, Stella. People will never accept them. People will never accept *you* if you defend them."

"There has to be. And I don't need you to find it. Gaspare will help me."

"Oh, it's 'Gaspare' now, is it? You've known him less than a week and already he's your savior?"

"Well, he is the leader of the free world, Gresham. He's pretty damned qualified. And he cares about me—I know he does. We're family. We don't have anyone else, but we have each other."

Gresham's face fell a moment before the clench left his fists. His shoulders sagged, and he took a step away from me. The look in his eyes was no longer fierce but—I almost thought—hurt. "You have no one? Is that what you think?" His eyes narrowed and he said just above a whisper, "You had me."

"Don't you dare, Rowan Gresham," I seethed. "Don't you dare try to make me feel bad. Not after the shit you've pulled, the secrets you've kept. I—"

"I've only ever tried to protect you," he interrupted.

"Protect me? Seems more and more all the time like I needed protection *from* you. Why keep my relation to Gaspare a secret? Tell me that. How could that possibly have been in my best interest?"

"Think for one second, Stella." He approached me until I could see the tiny black hairs on his square jaw. He'd gotten dangerously close to me. Too close. I backed away so I could think.

I couldn't come up with an answer to his question and threw my hands up.

Gresham huffed out a breath. "I hadn't told Gaspare everything about you because once I did the 'leader of the free world' would know your genealogy, your mother's history, and that you were a potential threat. You don't know him like you think you do. He didn't become the PM by being a nice guy. He sure as hell hasn't kept the job that way."

"What are you saying? Are you saying he's crooked? Violent?"

"Crooked? No. But he isn't the sweetheart you're making him out to be. He's a hardass with a keen grasp of the greater good. Care to guess what the greater good to the leader of Thayer is?" When I just scowled he went on. "No? *People.* The welfare of Thayer's people is his primary concern."

Neither of us said anything for a long time. I didn't know where to start, or if the argument was finished. "I have to go," I finally said. "I have a meeting."

"With Gaspare," Gresham ran a hand over the top of his head. "I know."

When I arrived at the prime minister's residence Paul was there to take me to the back gardens. The grounds had been designed for entertaining. Elegant hardscapes featured fountains, seating, and backdrops perfect for stages. Green expanses stretched behind the grounds.

It was on one of these greens that I found Gaspare.

My uncle clasped me by the shoulders and smiled when I approached. This was the hug of our current comfort level, I supposed. I was glad to see him and a smile lit my face, too.

"What do you think is the greatest advantage of being an omni, Stella?"

Straight to business, then. O-kay. "Gosh. I don't know. Besides the obvious choice of having any animal form at your disposal, you mean?"

He nodded somberly.

I blew out a breath as I contemplated his question. "I'm sorry. I just don't know."

"That's okay," he said and folded his hands behind his back. "That's why we're here."

I swallowed, but my mouth had gone dry. I hadn't anticipated he'd be so formal after the way he behaved the last we interacted.

"Power," he said and began to circle me. "Power, and lots of it, is the best thing about being an omni."

"Aha," I said, though I was far from a conclusion.

He stood in front of me and touched my face—the lightest press of his fingers to my temple. "May I?" he asked. I wasn't sure for what he was requesting permission, but I agreed with a nod nonetheless.

I felt a pull on my mind like taffy on teeth. It was warm, pliable. Not unpleasant, but unfamiliar. After a while, the pull lost its novelty, yet I was still left with something gunky. I shook my head and backed away. I tried to dislodge him from my brain but the harder I worked to eject him, the more crevices he melted into.

I cleared my throat, worked my shoulders, shook my head once more. I finally found my voice. "Gaspare. That's enough. I don't like it."

The tug on my mind snapped and I was free of him. The intrusion irritated me, and it must've shown on my face because he approached me in a rush. "Stella, I'm sorry. I assumed Gresham told you."

"He didn't. What'd you do?" I opened and closed my mouth, tried to pop my ears, to clear my head.

"I'm so sorry. I got inside your head. Saw some memories."

"You can do that?" *For god's sake*, I thought. *Would the extent of this nonsense never end? Was nothing sacred?*

"Yes. I can see memories, thoughts."

"Do you have to have permission, or were you just being polite?"

He inclined his head. He'd been polite. That was scary.

"What did you see?"

"I found what I went looking for. I wanted to see your childhood." He frowned. "It was lonelier than I expected."

I didn't like how that statement made me feel. "What else?"

"That's it. I saw some things as you saw them. A child's perspective."

"No, what else can you do? With this power you spoke of."

"Ah," he said. "I'll demonstrate." With the flick of his hand a crack formed in the greens between us. The crevice expanded until the trees nearby shuddered and swayed. It grew so wide I couldn't have jumped it if I tried.

I looked wildly to Gaspare, who stood grinning and relaxed. He twirled his hand again and the crevice closed together with a creak. It fit back together so seamlessly I'd never have been able to tell he'd torn it apart.

"You can move earth?" I said, hands firmly on my hips.

"A bit, yes."

"I don't suppose you can do any tricks with the heavens?"

"No," he laughed. "Just the stars."

"Just the— Are you freakin' kidding me?"

His goofy grin was infectious. "Mostly. Our power originates from the stars. Surely you know this." When I shook my head in bewilderment he scowled. "What are they teaching you at The Root?"

"Well, a lot of basics so far. Some practical information. Dean Miles says we're not yet competent enough to access any real power."

"Dean Miles? Oh, you mean Livia?" He snorted. "Livia wouldn't know true power if it knocked her on her frigid ass."

My laughter seemed to encourage him because he went on, "The only reason she has that job is due to her connection to Rowan. I'll never understand what he sees in her."

"You and me both. She's hateful as a sober spinster."

"That's precisely what she is!" Gaspare laughed and his face crinkled in all the right places. "Rowan swore he'd never remarry. All these years she thought she'd change his mind. But she's as stubborn as she is hateful."

"Remarry?" I leaned forward to hear him better. "Gresham was married? When? To whom?"

Gaspare straightened, a serious look pulling his mouth where the grin had been. "Not my story to tell. Not today." He looked at something beyond my shoulder. "Hi, Paul. Is he here?" I turned to see Paul nod. "All right. I'll be right in."

Gaspare seemed to operate on a breeze, the wind of responsibility always blowing him this way and that. He clasped my hands in his and squeezed. "Great start today, Stella. Same time Thursday?"

I smiled, shrugged, and squeezed back. "Thursday."

23

Timbra had been notably absent from her room over the last few days.

She hadn't come back to our suite at the cabin Saturday after the ordeal with Boone, either. I gave up waiting for her that night; assumed she and Boone had worked through their issues. Alone with my thoughts, I lay in the cabin's comfortable bed with the windows open and ran fingers over my lips recalling the sweetness, the emotion, the passion with which Ewan Bristol had kissed me. I fell asleep to the chorus of frogs calling to their mates near the crisp mountain lake.

By Tuesday I could contain my curiosity no longer.

"Wanna go into town for lunch today?" I asked Timbra during our eight-thirty Tools class. "I saw this great row of restaurants just off Caliph Square."

"Oh," she grimaced in apology. "I have plans with Boone."

"With Boone?" I asked too loudly and he whipped his head in our direction. I waved a dismissal at him and returned to Timbra. "You two've barely seen the light of day this week. Don't you think you can spare an hour for your girl?"

She stuck out her tongue at my shameless attempt to guilt her. "Of course I can. But if we run over an hour, you're buying." She smirked and pulled out her P.I.A., which she'd named Fawn. She made a dramatic show of adding our lunch date to her calendar. Then she obviously texted Boone because I heard his affronted huff before he shot me a playful stink-eye.

"So?" I said, once we were seated at a little bistro. "Are you gonna tell me what's up with you and Boone or do I have to divine it myself?"

"Ugh." She threw her head back. "I don't know what to say. We haven't discussed the topic of my dad. The only thing we've worked through is that we won't—can't live without each other. We want to be together, and that's what we're doing. We're happy. That's what's important."

"Oh, great," I said. "I'm so happy for you." I nodded and tried to leave the conversation at that.

"What?" Timbra's ears stiffened in defiance.

"Nothing." I shook my head. Blinked maybe a few too many times.

She took a bite of her veggie crepe.

I took a drink. Tried to mind my own business. "It's just—well, what about when your dad finds out? 'Cause he will. He did the first time."

She crossed lithe arms over her narrow chest. "He won't. We're so careful. We're making sure not to be seen alone together. We're not telling anyone we're together."

"Okay," I said and nodded.

"You don't think it'll work?" Her left ear gave the slightest twitch.

"I—" I stopped. Composed my thoughts. "I just don't think it's a long-term plan."

"I know that. We know that. But it's all I've got right now."

Though I'd worked hard not to ruffle her scruff, I'd still done it. "I'm sorry," I said. "I'm just trying to look out for you, to help you work through this."

"I know." She blinked and her long eyelashes lay on her high cheekbones.

For the first time, I noticed someone sitting at a corner table in the back. The table's occupant raised a hand to me.

Recognition dawned. *Stryde. Huh. What a coincidence.* He moved to rise and I widened my eyes at him, shook my head to indicate he shouldn't approach. Instead of remaining seated—and unnoticed—he lumbered to our table. I hadn't taken a breath since I'd seen him. I looked wildly to Timbra. Back to Stryde. *Closer. Closer.*

"Fancy meeting you here," he said and pasted on that same disfigured smile.

"Ah. Stryde. Hello. I…ah…didn't expect to see you here." I tilted my head in silent question. *What are you doing here?*

"Have you ladies had a nice lunch?" he asked. Just another day. Just another guy.

Timbra cleared her throat in an obvious attempt to be introduced.

I shook my head in defeat. "Stryde, this is my friend Timbra. Timbra…Stryde." Short and sweet because I had no idea how I would explain our association.

"Nice to meet you," she said. "How do you two know each other?"

I looked to the sky for help. To be struck by lightening. Something.

"Oh," I said. "Ah. I met Stryde with Gresham." It was true enough.

"Mind if I sit with you for a moment?" he asked. *Oh, for goodness sake.*

"Not at all," Timbra smiled pleasantly and indicated the chair beside her.

The next fifteen minutes were some of my most tense. I was sure that at any moment Stryde would reveal our connection, would expose himself as a dragon. Then what would I do? I had no idea. I was so sick and tired of secrets, but they were never ending. Timbra knew my secret, my mother's, even my father's. But the fact I was communicating with the Drakontos dragons was something I'd yet to reveal.

Timbra squinted at me several times; she knew something was off. I found somewhere else to look each time she tried to catch my attention. Finally, our check came. I couldn't get out of there fast enough.

"Goodbye, Stryde. It was good to see you. Tell your family hello for me," I said.

He grabbed me in an awkward bear hug. I grunted as he squeezed me into his chest, my chin jutting upward with the force of it. He looked down at me and his emerald eyes were crazed, overloaded. He was going to have to get some serious help with his social skills if he wanted to successfully reenter society. I was aware of his issues, had a personal connection, and still I found him creepy as hell.

Timbra backed up a step when he released me, her disinterest in such an embrace apparent in her rigid posture. "A pleasure to meet you," she said eloquently.

"Let's go," I grabbed her arm and traced back to The Root.

"What. The hell. Was that?" Timbra asked as we entered our History of Herbalism class.

"Just some weird guy I know," I said and changed the subject to one I knew she'd embrace. "I see Boone and Ewan."

She took the seat next to Boone and I scooted past them to the other side of Ewan, who looked fantastic in a tight black T-shirt. Black sneakers peeked beneath the legs of his faded jeans.

Once I was seated, Ewan leaned into me. "Hi," he said playfully. He smelled clean, of masculine soap, and I closed my eyes for the briefest moment to enjoy it without distraction. When his arm brushed mine the intense warmth he always radiated sent shivers down my spine.

"Hi yourself." I couldn't help the grin that took over my face. I didn't even try.

"You smell funny," he said after a moment.

"What?" I inconspicuously sniffed toward an armpit.

"I thought I caught a whiff of something…different. Strange." He leaned in farther and inhaled the air around my chest. The bold move stunned me and I gasped. Ewan opened his mouth and ran his tongue along the roof of his mouth; he was working to discern a scent. Then he stiffened. "Who've you been…touching?"

"Touching?" The day's events sped through my mind. "I don't—I don't know."

His smile turned to a scowl in record time. Suspicion and restraint tensed his square jaw. "You smell like a male. A strange one. One I don't know." A rumble erupted from low in his chest.

"Oh!" I put fingers to my forehead. "I saw someone I knew at lunch. He hugged me. Very awkward, actually. Wish he hadn't." The growl grew louder and the professor shot us a warning look.

"What is he?" Ewan said just above a whisper.

"What is—oh. He's an…um…reptile of some sort. Alligator maybe?"

"Not alligator, no." He shook his head, his eyes menacing slits. "I don't recognize this scent. Reptilian in a way. But…like embers somehow. Not woodsmoke. Almost like fire itself. He smells a lot like you—"

He didn't finish his thought. Ewan Bristol had always been far too perceptive.

The pace of my breaths increased until I began to pant. I didn't say a word, and I couldn't—wouldn't look at Ewan. I stared straight ahead, my mind working furiously to determine what to do. He'd figure it out, if he hadn't already.

"You. Me. My place after class," he demanded. When I bristled and began to protest he stared me down. Dared me to refuse. To deny it. I couldn't and he knew it. I heaved a breath and looked back toward the instructor, but my thoughts were a thousand miles away.

Ewan's room was tidy and his bed was made. Books and magazines lay neatly on the table. I ran my fingers along the even tops of them; idly rifled through the literary magazine on top.

"Sit," he ordered. I clenched my jaws, but took the corner chair, which was more tattered than the one in my room. "Explain."

I looked up at him. His face was severe, his handsome features tightly leashed. I closed my eyes in defeat, in dread. The moment I closed them my face shot hot with emotion. My cheeks tightened and pinched just before tears stung my eyes.

I couldn't stand the thought of Ewan knowing about my mother, about the Drakontos dragons. About *me*. It wasn't just the fear he'd lose interest in me; I feared losing his respect. He'd become a pivotal figure in my life, and I didn't want to lose that. I turned my head in shame, hid my face with my hand.

There was no halting the sobs that wracked my body. They came dark and forceful like a wall of storm clouds. They wouldn't be stopped until they'd drenched every last thing in their path.

I sat in Ewan's threadbare chair and dissolved completely into the singular mess in his tidy room.

Ewan didn't come to me; he didn't comfort me. He didn't insist I stop crying or tell me to grow up. He offered nothing at all.

Once I'd had my release and could think beyond my own misery, I looked up to find him sitting on the edge of the bed. He'd watched silently as I fell to pieces.

I sniffed and sat up straight. Cleared my throat. "Not much on sympathy, are you?" I found a tissue in my pocket and wiped my nose.

"I have two sisters. Tears'll not derail me from what I want to know."

"I wasn't trying to derail anything. I'm upset. I never wanted to have this conversation with you."

"Why not?" He sat unmoving on the bed. Rigid. If I didn't know better, I'd think he was as opposed to talking about it as I was.

"Because. My mother was who she was. Because I'm who I am."

"And who was your mother?" He took a deep breath. "Who are you?"

I closed my eyes again. Breathed. Forced them open. Breathed. Willed the words to leave my mouth.

"Tell me, Stella," he said. His voice was low, smooth. His expression was hollow, devoid of emotion.

"Edina," I breathed.

"Edina?" His face pinched in incomprehension, drawing his dark brows together and throwing shadows over his eyes.

"The only one you know. The one from the stories." His eyes widened at my words, and his nostrils flared before rejoining his slim nose. For an eternity he just looked at me. Not moving. Not speaking. Barely breathing. The intensity with which he studied me was frightening.

"And you?" he said after a time. "Who are you?"

"I'm half dragon, Ewan. I'm the daughter of a killer. I'm the girl people are gonna *love* to hate." My lips quivered and my despair threatened to take control once more. I sat up straighter. *No. I will not break down again,* I demanded of myself.

Never taking his gaze from mine, Ewan rose from the bed. He bent his knees, his back still straight and strong, and knelt in front of me. I felt the warmth of his long arms as he pushed them along my thighs and around my hips. Ewan pulled me into him, forcing my legs on either side of his waist.

We were at eye level and he stared into mine as he slowly shook his head.

"No," he said, putting the full force of his gaze, of his bearing, behind his words. "No. You're Stella Stonewall and that's what matters. I've known who you are since first I laid eyes on you. And I like it. Very much. *Too much.*" His voice rasped with emotion. "You're determined, and you work hard. You're kind, generous. You're the smartest person I know. You're good, Stella—I know that like I know myself."

"Ewan," I whispered and threw my arms around him. "You don't know what you're saying. I could be dangerous. And I'm not just talking physically. Politically, too. Being known as my friend could mean serious trouble for you."

"Funny," he said. He pulled back and kissed high on my cheekbone where my tears had been moments before. "I forgot to add that you're funny."

I let out a sad chuckle. "You confound me, Ewan Bristol. You absolutely blow my mind."

I leaned forward to eliminate the few inches that separated us and kissed Ewan's full mouth. My lips dissolved into his, and with them my body melted, too. I used my legs to pull him tighter into me. He got my meaning and jerked my hips roughly against him. My fingers found their way to his springy curls, something I'd been dying to do. I grasped big handfuls of his hair and steered his head toward the ceiling for access to his neck. His perpetual five o'clock shadow had called to me since the moment I met him. I ran my lips and then my cheek along the scruff, delighting in the rasp. When I pressed my lips to the little hollow at the bottom of his throat, I felt the vibrations of his rumbled pleasure and my lips abandoned their pursed position for a grin.

His hands were just under the waistband of my jeans and he trailed his fingers lightly along the top of my ass. I pulled back to see his face, intent on finding his lips. His eyes held undeniable heat, but something more, too.

I took his lips again, but his response was measured. He didn't deny me, but he didn't reciprocate. I pulled back to search his eyes as my heart showed the early signs of ache. It was tight, strained. Not pained yet, but close.

"What's wrong?" I whispered. "You having second thoughts?" The pressure on my heart grew and I had difficulty pulling in my breaths. "It's okay if you are. I understand. I know this situation is—"

"You didn't tell me who the guy was," he said. He'd pulled his hands back to his own knees, his posture rigid once more.

"The guy?"

"The one I smelled. The one who smells like you do."

I couldn't get anything past him. "Ah. Ok. Well." I heaved out a breath. Stalled. "Ah..."

"It's one of them, isn't it? The dragons from the crater with Brandubh?"

I could only nod my head.

"Dammit, Stella!" The volume, the fury in his voice was unexpected, and I jumped. "What the hell are you thinking? Who is he? Are you seeing him, too? Have we gotten nowhere?" He stood and backed away from me. "Am I still competing for you?" he asked, then began to pace within the confines of his room. "Is this about power, Stella—who's the biggest alpha male? It's not Gresham now, but some male dragon I have to compete with?"

"What? Wait. No," I shook my head. "I don't care about that. It's not likc that."

"What's it like, then?"

"God, Ewan. He's my cousin. The three dragons from the crater that day are my mother's family."

"Fuck," he said and sat roughly onto his bed.

"You can say that again."

"Fuck," he breathed.

24

By Thursday, I was looking forward to seeing my uncle Gaspare again. Classes that day were both fun and insightful, Ewan seemed to be working toward accepting my reality (at least his face wasn't frowning and broody every time I looked at him), and a cool breeze provided relief from the day's heat.

I should've known things were too good to be true.

As we left our last class for the day, Timbra's P.I.A. gave a loud alert from her shoulder bag.

"What is it, Fawn?" she asked the device.

"Timbra, you've received a request to report to the registrar's office at once."

She looked to the group and most of us shrugged. We had no idea what was going on. We hadn't received the same requests.

"Do you know why?" Timbra asked.

"Your account indicates you've been dis-enrolled from Radix," Fawn intoned. "Perhaps the two have some correlation."

"Dis-enrolled," she repeated. "By whom?"

"Mr. Russet Redfern," the device replied.

The blood drained from Timbra's face and her pert ears fell with it. She was stunned, bereft. Her mouth opened, but she didn't move or speak.

"I'll go with you," Boone said and ran his arm across her back. "I'll talk to him. We'll get this sorted out."

"No," she croaked and shook herself. "No. I'll go. I made the decision to be with you. I'll face the consequences."

"But…but... You can't leave The Root," Layla said. "No one gets *in* The Root. Surely he wouldn't pull you out; deny you this great opportunity just because you're dating Boone."

"Oh, he would." Timbra's voice, her posture, everything about her was flat. Defeated. "And he obviously has."

Timbra returned to her room, and I knocked before entering through our shared bathroom.

"Come in." She had opened a large navy blue trunk, and its gold locking device rattled each time she threw something into it.

"What are you doing?" I knew what she was doing, but couldn't accept it.

"Packing. Leaving. He really did it," Timbra said as she transferred a stack of shirts from her dresser to the trunk.

"You can't leave. No." Tears stung my eyes and spilled onto my face before the words left my mouth.

"It's okay, Stella," she said. "I don't really belong here anyway. I mean, how can a doe defend Thayer? We're not even a very magical people. How can I ever put to use what we're learning? My mom never attended The Root. I was shocked when my father agreed to let me come. He's pretty old fashioned, you may have noticed."

"I'll talk to him. Maybe he'll listen to someone else? Maybe if he got to know Boone?" I was reaching, and we both knew it.

"It's over, sweetie," she said. "There's nothing to be done about it."

"No," I whispered and fell into her chair.

She set down the picture frame she'd been holding. "You can visit me anytime, Stell. That's the great thing about tracing. Need your friend? Just pop over after class." Her ears stiffened with anger. "My father's had me banned from campus, so I'm afraid I can't join you at Sabre or along the food court."

"And Boone?" I asked.

"I'll end it with Boone. For good. There's no way it can work, my father's right."

"Oh, Timbra. I'm so sorry."

She twisted her mouth, tried not to cry. "It'll be fine. In time. You're going to be late."

"Late? Oh! My meeting with Gaspare. He'll understand."

"I will not have you late to your meeting with the PM on my account. Get." When I didn't move she cocked her head at me. "I'm serious. Go. I promise we can meet on Saturday for lunch. You can come out to my house, check up on me."

"Okay," I conceded and stood to leave. "I love you, Timbra Redfern. And I hate this whole thing."

She wrapped her willowy body around me and squeezed. "Me too."

25

"Something's different about you today," Gaspare said and stepped away from me. We were studying the body compositions of various animals so that I could better control their forms. Though I could manage at least the basics of flight in my dragon form, manipulating smaller birds was a real challenge. My natural inclination was to operate them like I would my dragon, which was gross over-maneuvering and caused me to flail wildly through the air. I suffered more than a few hard landings, and had the scrapes and bruises to prove it.

Gaspare searched my face, scanned my body. "Have you been hurt?"

I gave a sad laugh. "Not in the way you mean."

He set down the model he'd been holding. "What's going on?"

I felt stupid telling such an important man about my problems at school. About my BFF's breakup with her forbidden boyfriend. "Nothing important. Just some stuff at The Root. It's not important."

"Is it important to you?" he asked and sank onto a tufted leather ottoman.

"Of course. She's my best friend. She's wonderful, and so is Boone. The whole thing is bullshit and I cannot believe her dad pulled her out of The Root."

"Wait, wait, wait," Gaspare said, and held up his hands. His blue eyes gleamed with repressed mirth at my information dump. "Start from the beginning. Who is 'she'?"

"Sorry. Timbra Redfern. She's my suite mate and my dearest friend. Her dad's Russet Redfern. I met him once. He's an overbearing asshole that treats Timbra like chattel—Oh. My goodness. I'm sorry. I tend to lose control of my mouth when I get excited."

He laughed and waved away my concern. "Russ Redfern? I've known Russ for a long time. Why has he pulled his daughter from Radix?"

I told him Boone and Timbra's entire story—about their forbidden but inescapable love.

"I can see why Russ was so upset," he said. When I bristled he stopped me. "But, I've learned a thing or two about taboo relationships." He raised an eyebrow at me. "They can have gloriously unexpected outcomes. They can result in gifts you never imagined, but treasure above all others."

He was referring to me, to my parents' forbidden love.

My heart jumped toward him and my body followed. I squeezed him in a hug so tight and unexpected that he grunted.

"I'm sorry about your friend," he said.

I twisted my lips and nodded my head in thanks.

"Now let's get to work. I thought today we could work on flying."

"That's all right, Stella. Try again." Gaspare had been extremely patient with me as I attempted to refine my aerial skills.

"Ugh!" I growled, beyond frustrated. I couldn't get past the neophytic and mechanical winging I'd first developed. Getting airborne was no problem; neither was going forward, but compared to Gaspare's effortless and beautiful aeronautics, my movements were crude and stunted.

"Listen," he said. "I know you're used to excelling at whatever you try, and that's a good thing. But when it comes to flying, you can't think it into perfection. You can't pull all-nighters until you memorize it. Flying is an instinct, a calling; it's a release of control."

"I'm trying," I whined. "I really am."

"I know you are," he said. His steel-blue eyes were kind but determined. "And maybe that's your problem—you're over-thinking it. What you must do is just…let go. As an omni you have the natural ability to change forms mid-flight. I cannot express enough the usefulness of this property in a fight.

"But it's so much more than an offensive weapon. The freedom to meld one form to another is something I could never describe to you. Like learning to allow your instincts to guide your flight instead of your brain, it's indescribable. It's something only you can discover."

He was right, of course. My way certainly wasn't working. But 'letting go' mid-flight hundreds of feet above the ground was…well, it was about as hard as it sounds.

"You'll get it," Gaspare assured me. "You'll get it. You just need practice."

But I wasn't feeling very hopeful.

"When do I learn to breathe fire?" I asked.

"What?"Gaspare's head turned to the side as he tried to determine my meaning. "Breathe fire? Ohhhh. Yes. I hadn't thought of that. It's not something I can help you with."

"Why not?"

"Well, I have no frame of reference."

"But as an omni, you can change into a dragon."

"That's true. But a dragon's fire is a magic that belongs solely to…her. I can take the form, it's true, but I cannot produce a flame."

"No kidding," I breathed. "Well, how will I learn? Then again, being bi-species, maybe I don't even have the ability."

"Besides discovering it yourself, I'm afraid I can't help you. It's unfortunate you have no one to serve as a mentor—at least in this."

"Yes," I said. "That's too bad."

I arrived at the Drakontos' cabin to find it eerily quiet.

"Bay?" I called, toeing around the property. "Uncle Eiven? Stryde?"

I wandered outside the wooden structure and inspected the dusty fire pit and Bay's prolific garden. Just as I reached to touch what would become a lovely purple heirloom tomato, the turbulence of something huge and fast overhead sent my body rigid with fear. A warm, wet substance trailed down my wrist, and I looked to find the fruit squashed in my hand. *What a waste*, I thought and dove for the fertile dirt.

With my back to the ground, I could better see what caused such a commotion. Three dragons the size of Cessnas rolled and swooped gracefully through the blue sky. I envied the ease with which they navigated flight.

Eiven spotted me and dove low. A helpless yelp escaped my open mouth as I crab-crawled away from the gigantic red dragon closing in on me at high speed. Closer…closer. *Too close!*

Just before impacting the ground near the house, Eiven rolled and stood on two human feet. I heaved a sigh of relief and fell onto my butt in the dirt.

Eiven snagged a pair of work pants lying near the shed and was clothed when he exited the other side of the dilapidated building. Bay followed, her landing no less breathtaking. The shed must've served as an informal dressing room, for Bay aimed for the shanty, too, and found a worn cotton dress.

As Stryde hit the ground his muscular human form rippled into existence. He wasn't in as much of a hurry to find his clothes as Eiven and Bay had been. I suspected he was showing off as he strutted toward the outbuilding. Instead of grabbing his jeans right away he stretched long tanned arms above his head and arched his chiseled back. I caught him watching from the corner of his eye to see if I watched. *O-kay…*

"Stella, what a nice surprise," Bay said. "We were just getting some exercise. Come on in the house, dear." I found the same spot at the kitchen table I'd occupied the last time.

"Back for the beer, eh?" Eiven winked and the wrinkles at the corners of his eyes squeezed happily into each other.

"Oh, that does sound great," I said. "Thank you."

Eiven busied himself with pint glasses and Bay twisted her gray hair into a loose bun at the crown of her head. Stryde had managed to locate his clothes and strolled inside, too.

"Actually," I continued. "I…I have some questions. About myself. About dragons. And, well, since I don't know any other dragons, I hoped you could help me."

"Of course we can," Bay said at the same time Stryde said, "What do you want to know?"

My thin gold bracelets clinked lightly together as I ran my fingers over them, gathering my thoughts. "I'm having trouble flying," I finally said. All three of my relatives cocked their heads so similarly it was comical. "I mean, of course I can fly. You've seen me do that. But I can't maneuver as gracefully as you all do."

"It takes time. You've just begun. Don't worry about that," Eiven said and passed me a pint of the amber nectar.

"There's more. I've accepted that I'm a dragon, embraced it, even. But I have no idea how to breathe fire. And, well, that's a basic function of someone like us, I'd think. Can you help me?"

"I'd be honored to help you," Stryde said formally.

Bay and Eiven eyed each other, and Bay hastily cleared her throat. "We'll all help," she said. "Be glad to."

"*This is more difficult than I thought it'd be,*" Eiven said after attempting to explain the technical logistics of dragon fire. "*I've been calling fire for so long it's second nature.*"

"*For me, too.*" Bay's lovely but fierce brown dragon was the color of a bomber jacket. "*Perhaps we should try to pinpoint from where it first originates so we can better describe it to her.*"

"*Mmm. A good idea,*" Eiven agreed, and Stryde nodded his onyx head.

The three dragons took turns firing columns of fire across the open sky. It was a good thing their hideout was so secluded. There was no way the pyrotechnics could be dismissed if we were in town.

Watching them experiment was an experience in itself. Not only were they fearsome and exotically beautiful, they were having fun. Eiven playfully shot a plume at Stryde, who whipped around in fury. He snarled angrily at his dad, who threw his head back and barked a laugh. *Now there's a sight I never thought to see,* I thought. *A chuckling dragon. Sounds like the morning after bad Chinese.*

Eiven's dry laugh wheezed and I realized he'd heard my thoughts. I grinned at him, something that came surprisingly easy even in my dragon form.

"*I think I've pinpointed it,*" called Bay. "*Yes. That's definitely it.*" She coughed after a singe sputtered and died in her great mouth. "*I'll meet you at that clearing. I think she'll have more luck if she's not concentrating on flying and finding her flame at the same time.*"

"*The important thing to understand,*" Bay said once we'd gathered in the clearing, "*is that you're manipulating two separate mechanisms. One to supply the fuel, and the other to ignite it.*"

Eiven and Stryde nodded their heads in comprehension. I nodded, too, though I hoped she'd expound on her statement.

"*Ah. Okay. I assume locating the fuel line would be a good place to start?*" I asked.

"*Precisely,*" Bay said. "*This is something you'll only ever find in your form, dear, do you understand?*" I made an attempt to shrug my dragon shoulders, but the movement was jerky and inadequate. Luckily she went on, "*A dragon's fire is magic—extraordinary, singular magic, for only a dragon possesses it.*"

This I'd heard before. "*Go on,*" I said.

"*When walking on two feet you'll not have access to your fire. No other species can acquire or replicate it. 'Tis a magic all our own,*" she said with gravity. "*Dragons' magic.*"

"*It's one of the reasons we're superior, feared,*" intoned Stryde, who seemed far more at home in his dragon skin than that of a man. "*But also the reason we've been desired as weapons.*"

"*I see.*" I nodded soberly.

Bay shook herself. It was obvious that teaching me about fire without getting bogged down in the past was extremely difficult. "*Deep inside your dragon lies this magic,*" she said. "*Untapped until you seek it out, until you draw it into your powerful chest and choose to expel it.*"

"*Maybe I don't have it,*" I mused. "*Maybe because I'm only half, the dragon magic didn't pass on to me.*"

"*The only way to know is to try.*" Bay nodded her encouragement.

"*Okay.*" Her descriptions were helpful. I searched within myself for some great magic lying in wait for my request. I ran an imaginary hand over those nuclei of power I'd already discovered—my chakra, my heart, my mind. But it wasn't there.

A rumble low in my stomach alerted me to hunger pangs. I ducked my head in embarrassment. I really wasn't prepared to think about what dragons ate. No thank you. I much preferred waiting to have a sandwich back at The Root.

When I looked up from my traitorous belly I found Eiven's eyes alight with pride. "*You've found it,*" he said reverently.

"*Huh?*"

"*It's there,*" Stryde said. "*The magic. Stored deep in your bowels. Can you access it again?*"

"*I'll try,*" I said and mentally dove to the depths of my scaled belly. It was full, ready, like if I just squeezed hard enough something would shoot straight up through my esophagus. I gave a mental "*Whoop!*" at my success, and the three other dragons cheered.

"*Excellent, dear,*" Bay said. "*Now to ignite it.*"

That sounded more dangerous. I looked to each of them nervously, but their faces were supportive, expectant. It was the best chance I had at learning to manipulate the form, the magic I was born with. No reason not to take it. I released the breath I'd been holding since Bay uttered the word 'ignite.' "*Let's do this*," I said.

Bay had difficulty explaining the second component. After several attempts, she let Eiven take the reins.

"*Have you ever seen a flint rock?*" he asked, his red scales glowing like banked embers in the setting sun.

"*I have*, yes."

"*Good. Imagine your throat is made of flint.*"

"*O-kayyyy.*" That was easier said than done.

"*Just go with it*," he said with a reptilian grin. I nodded. "*Now, if your throat were made of flint and you squeezed it forcefully together what would happen?*"

"*Ah, well, I guess it might produce a spark?*"

"*Yes!*" Stryde yelped enthusiastically, earning him a startled look from all of us. He'd been eerily quiet during the teaching process. He scrutinized us—well, me—intently as I tried to grasp the concepts.

"*Ah, good*," Eiven continued. "*So, if you could release some of the magical fuel from your belly, and then quickly squeeze your flinted throat together, what then?*"

"*Fire*," I said with force. "*I could shoot flames.*"

"*You could*," he nodded his great head. "*You can.*"

And, dammit, I believed I could! I had to try.

"*All right*," I said. "*Back up. I've no idea how this will turn out.*"

The three dragons folded in behind me, and the strength, the energy of their support was palpable. Facing the widest part of the clearing, my scaled chest expanded on a soul-deep breath. I imagined unscrewing the gas cap of the fuel line in my stomach and releasing its powerful fumes.

Nothing happened.

The fullness, the potential remained. But nothing came out.

"*S'all right, dear*," Bay said. "*Try again.*"

I did. And when I did, a fissure formed in the lining of my fuel tank. The tiniest amount of gaseous magic escaped my innards and found its way up the back of my throat. It tasted of magic; of fire itself.

The discovery pleased me so much that the fuel evaporated before it occurred to me to strike the flint of my esophagus. I let out an exasperated growl that, in my dragon form, expelled as a roar that reverberated through the clearing and shook the saplings around us.

"*Oops.*"

"*You'll get it,*" Eiven coaxed. "*I know you'll get it. This is a great start.*"

After several more attempts I succeeded in learning to release the gaseous fuel, but was never able to make a spark.

Bay, Eiven and Stryde assured me my fire would come in time, and invited me back to practice.

"*We've all the time in the world,*" Eiven said. "*We'll help you find it.*"

They asked me to stay for dinner, but the thought of food turned my stomach. The many explorations into my stomach, metaphysical or not, left me nauseous.

26

I returned to my room at Sabre, but without Timbra next door everything was…wrong. I couldn't stand the quiet. I left for the bustle of the bar.

Ewan, Raynor, Layla, and Boone sat at our usual table. The first three were making plans for the weekend but Boone sat silent, introspective. His big body slumped in the club chair and he looked more miserable than I felt.

He didn't look up when I took a seat. His big hand dwarfed my own when I gave it an encouraging squeeze. He looked up then, his blue eyes rimmed with red, and so very pained. He released a lopsided smile, like only half of him could even produce the effort to try.

Mari buzzed up to our table for my order and gave Layla a quick wink. Layla smiled back so brightly I hoped it might light up Boone a bit. Mari flitted back toward the bar, breezy as ever, and gave Knox the order. I waved when he looked in my direction. He nodded and grinned, and was caught by one of the barstools' occupants. She whipped around in her seat to see who'd received it. My biggest fan. Dean Miles. I waved at her, too. Maybe overly-friendly. Maybe a bit spitefully. *Screw her, though,* I thought. *I am so over this day.*

After a bit of small talk I could contain my curiosity no longer and leaned toward Layla. "I came by your room last week to see if you wanted to snag dinner."

"Oh?" she said and quirked a pierced brow. "Was I not there? I hate I missed it."

"You were there all right. But not alone, so I left."

She pulled her lips toward her ears in an "eek" gesture before grinning.

"It wasn't Mari," I said. "She was working here."

Layla's grin fell and she shrugged. She didn't say anything.

"It's obvious she's crazy about you. And I know you like her, too."

"I do," she said emphatically.

"O-kay," I said, issuing myself a firm reminder to stay out of her business.

Musicians.

Friday's classes crept by. Not a single thing the professors said filtered to my brain. My thoughts were absorbed by my leggy, doe-eyed friend. The idea of sitting with someone else seemed traitorous, so I sat alone in the back row. My classmates began to file past me; class was over.

"Hey, Stell," Ewan called as I trudged across the leafy campus.

A large maple tree provided some much-needed shade. "Hi." I tried to be upbeat.

"You doin' okay?" he asked, and ran confident fingers from my elbow down to my hand before clasping it to his.

My sad smile was inescapable. "Not really. Just sucks. I miss my friend. This place isn't the same without her."

"I know," he nodded and a brown curl fell onto his smooth forehead. "Boone's a wreck. Hell, I miss her, too. I had an idea. I thought we could all get out of town tonight and invite Timbra. We could have a party in her honor."

I stood a little straighter; perked a tiny bit. "What are you thinking?"

"Layla's offered to bring her band for a song or two at the cabin. My sister agreed. There's a perfect spot on the back patio. We can invite a few people and I'll man the grill."

It was lucky Ewan was both strong and agile enough to catch me because I jumped at him. He grunted at my tight squeeze, but breathed a masculine sigh at the kiss I placed on the soft skin above his scruffy beard.

I couldn't contain a giggle as I slid to my feet, but left my arms around him. "Thank you," I said and put the full force of my emotions behind a kiss. He lifted me tightly against him and walked me back to the maple tree, pinning me against it.

"You're welcome," he whispered against my ear before playfully nipping it.

Shivers shot from my earlobe to my pinky toe, and I gently bucked toward him. He flashed that wolfish smile and closed in on me.

I loved kissing Ewan Bristol. It was never rushed; never forced. I luxuriated in his soft lips, the slow and sensual rubs of his tongue, the heat of his body against mine.

We were making out in the middle of The Root campus, of this I was aware. But I just couldn't find a reason to care.

Fine, I thought, *let all those bitches see who Ewan Bristol belongs to. Mine. He's* mine.

Ewan's sharp intake of breath and flare of passion as he pushed himself harder against me clued me in to the fact he'd heard my thoughts.

Oh hell—I didn't mean for you to—oh hell.

He never replied. Well, not with words. He held me so tightly I thought I'd lose consciousness. He kissed my eyes, my cheeks, the tip of my nose. He was supremely happy, and I would be lying if I said I didn't feel the same way.

That is, until I opened my eyes and saw the bulging eyes, the flared nostrils, the positively enraged face of Rowan Gresham. I pulled away from Ewan in reflex, looked down to make sure I wasn't exposing any skin, and when I lifted my eyes toward Gresham again, he was gone.

"I'll get the party started," Ewan said. "Right?"

He hadn't seen Gresham.

My nod was distracted.

"You go get Timbra. See you at the cabin," he said and smacked me soundly on the lips.

"Pia?"

"Ho, ho! Look who decided to talk to her P.I.A. Let me guess: you need to use my Contacts function," Pia said snidely. "What wish can I grant you today, Master?"

"Ha-freakin-ha, Pia. Haven't we already gone over this? I thought we established that I love you. I need you. Life would be but a wade through a low-brow sludge pile if not for your generous and frequent gifts of intellect and humor."

"Oh, stop," Pia said. "All right. Your assistant kissing is acceptable. I forgive you."

Sometimes she was so not worth the effort.

With Pia's help I found Timbra's home contact information and called her. Her voice was dead, flat. Her tone never rose above desolate when she agreed to let me visit.

Since I'd never been to her home, tracing straight there was impossible. And because her father had officially barred her from The Root, she couldn't come get me. We agreed to meet in Caliph Square and go together.

I was glad to see her and rushed in for a hug. She gave a half-ass effort at reciprocating. Surely she was allowed a little self pity, though it was the first glimpse of it I'd ever gotten. "Come on," I said. "Let's go back to your house. Show me where they're keeping you." It was a joke, but her frown deepened. Probably too close to the truth.

"I've got a surprise for you," I sang.

Her little ears perked a bit. Not much.

"Come on. I'll tell you all about it when we get there. You're gonna love it."

She nodded, clasped my hand, and after one frigid gust we stood just outside the gate of Timbra's family homestead. She'd once told me they were a farm family, but the size of their operation was shocking. A white two-story farmhouse was flanked by half a dozen barns and storage buildings that housed harvested crops, supplies, and gargantuan red farm equipment. The house itself was surrounded by fruit trees, and tall stalks of grass that rippled in the breeze.

Movement at the front of the house caught my eye as Timbra's father exited the front door and held it for someone. It wasn't her mother, but another man. My head flew back in disbelief when I recognized him. *What? Why would he be here?*

Gaspare Shaw extended a distinguished hand to Russ Redfern, who anxiously shook it. Russ didn't bow before him, but he came close. It was satisfying to see the overbearing bully practically cower to my uncle, I admit it.

The two never noticed Timbra and I, and Gaspare was gone before we could approach him.

"What was he doing here?" I whispered.

"I don't know. He arrived a while before I left. My father's very involved in politics, in agriculture policy. Maybe something to do with that."

"Huh." It was all I could manage to say as we headed toward the house.

When Russ saw Timbra, his eyes, which had been wide with pleasure, reduced to determined slits.

"What now?" she muttered, but then jerked her head up to make sure he hadn't heard her.

"Timbra. Good. I want to speak with you."

His tall frame was devoid of antlers this time, at least, though he was still imposing, and very nearly regal. He never noticed I was there. Certainly, he never acknowledged my presence.

Bet that'd change if you knew the niece of the man whose ass you were just kissing was standing right here, I thought.

"It's come to my attention that you showed great aptitude for diplomacy during your time at Radix," Russ was saying.

Timbra's mouth worked to form a response, but none came. His statement was surprising to me, too, though not unfounded. Her abilities as a leader were countless. She was clever, knowledgeable, tactful, thoughtful, great looking—yeah, I could totally see her excelling in politics…like her father.

Russ didn't meet her eyes when he said, "I fear I've made a mistake in withdrawing you. I'm re-enrolling you. You can start Monday."

Timbra still hadn't said a word. She stared at her father. Squinted as she tried to understand. Just as he turned to leave she said, barely above a whisper, "And what about Boone?"

I tried to find somewhere else to direct my attention; I was an intruder.

"The dog?" he scoffed. "I remain unmoved on that point. You'll not associate with him." He stepped toward Timbra, leaned over her in an obvious attempt to intimidate her. "Are we clear?"

Timbra's chest rose, and her spine straightened on an inhale. "Oh, we're clear," she said. "At least I am. I'm not returning to The Root."

Russ jerked at her words.

"Oh, you're not?" He smirked.

"No," she said firmly. "No, *sir.* If you forbid me from being with Boone, I'll not go back to school. Simple as that."

Timbra Redfern walked past her father and through the red front door of her family home. Russ's mouth was agape as he watched her leave. When he noticed me and squinted angrily, I shut my own open mouth and scuttled in behind her.

We sat in her upstairs bedroom, which was tastefully decorated in white and robin's egg blue. She didn't say anything for a long time; her mind was clearly a thousand miles away.

I ducked to find her gaze, which had been focused on the hardwood floor for far too long. "Want some good news?"

"Yes," she said with feeling.

"We're having a party tonight. For you. At Ewan's cabin in the woods. Layla's playing. It's gonna be awesome."

"And Boone? Will he be there?"

I wasn't sure what answer she was looking for, but gave the truthful one. "Ah. Yes?"

"Good," she said with a satisfied, and borderline deviant, smile. "Good."

We talked about The Root, her childhood, her room. I told her how much we missed her already.

"Timbra?" a willowy woman in her late fifties called as she pushed open the door. She was lovely. Fabulously put together, an older version of Timbra. "Oh, hello," she said when she saw me. "I didn't realize anyone was here. I'm Grace Redfern."

"Mother, this is Stella, the one I told you about." Timbra somehow found a smile as she introduced me.

Grace rushed toward me and enveloped me in squeeze. "Timbra has gone on and on about you. What a pleasure to finally meet you."

Her enthusiasm embarrassed me, and I made eyes at Timbra, who shrugged and looked at her mom with adoration. My heart swelled to see it. No wonder Timbra turned out so well, despite her asshole of a father.

"I'll make sure all of your things are clean to take back to Radix on Monday," Grace said as she went about the room picking up and sniff-testing pieces of clothing.

"Oh, no, Mom," Timbra shook her head. "I'm not going back."

"But your father said—"

"Dad said a condition of going back was not associating with Boone. And I won't do it, Mom. I can't." Her voice broke with emotion.

Grace took a seat on the bed and rubbed Timbra's youthful hands between her own. "I know how you feel about this boy," she said. "And I understand. It's not ideal." She swallowed hard. "No, it's not ideal at all." Her breath shuddered as it left her body, but she sat up straighter. "But one can hardly control how they feel. And marrying the 'right' man doesn't always work out perfectly, either."

She smoothed Timbra's hair from her head with a manicured hand. "But the fact is your father's a very shrewd man. He no doubt sees the benefits to having someone in the PM's office as greater than fighting this battle over a boy with you right now. He's backed off of his stance on you and Boone."

Timbra leaned back to study her mother's face. "What? I don't understand."

"Prime Minister Shaw came here—himself—today to ask that your father put you back in school. Promised you a spot on his staff once you've graduated."

I heard nothing after that. The women, the room, the world went silent and white. Gaspare had done this. For me. I closed my eyes, so grateful for him, for Timbra, for that day.

27

"Well, you clean up all right."

Timbra looked better than all right. She was fabulous in a strapless azure party dress. She'd dressed me in a sparkly gold top, a black pencil skirt, and gold heels. I was feeling pretty fabulous myself.

We stood just outside the wolf-emblazoned doors of Ewan's "cabin" and could hear Layla's band warming up out back. I anxiously lifted the bronze knocker. In a matter of seconds, Ewan swung the door wide and caught me up in his arms. He pressed his lips to mine and the scent, the heat of him washed over me like a ripple of love. I grinned so wide my cheeks hurt. *Me. Grinning. About a boy.*

"Well this is new," Timbra said with a wry turn of her mouth. I raised my shoulders in a helpless shrug. There was really no explaining it anyway.

"You look amazing," Ewan said as his gaze swept me from head to toe. "You look nice too, Timbra. Let's go. Everyone's dying to see you."

As we made our way through the expansive house, the blond wood of its interior was airy and open. The faint undertones of the wood structure, combined with occasional drifts of the vegetables grilling outside, smelled like home. My outlook elevated to damn-near ecstatic. My heart was full, and I was happy.

We joined the party through the open French doors leading to the back patio and pool. Someone had strung lights, and they swayed in the evening breeze, throwing streams of light like tiny, subdued disco balls.

Timbra stopped in her tracks when she saw how many had gathered for the party. She smiled widely when she saw our close friends were there: Layla and Mari, Raynor, Bex. Several others from The Root, too, as well as Loryn and her husband, Sterling, and some of their friends.

Timbra scanned the crowd until she found Boone, and her legs shot forward, dragging her body with them. She ran to him, wrapped her arms around his neck. He was stunned but quickly squeezed her to him. His wide blue eyes filled with tears in front of us all, but he didn't care. Neither did she. None of us could look away, and we watched the scene unfold like a telenovella as he kissed her fawn hair and lay his cheek against her head.

But his forehead folded in confusion when she stepped away from him and cleared her throat. Timbra took a deep breath, stood to her full height.

"I have some news," she announced and twisted her hands nervously. "This is a celebration. I'm returning to The Root."

Boone's mouth fell open and then formed into questions, "What? How?"

"My father's agreed to send me back. And even if he hadn't, I was coming back to you. I'd have found an apartment, a job, some way to be in the city."

"And us?" Boone whispered. His eyes shot back and forth between Timbra's as he awaited her answer. "What about us?"

Timbra nodded and smiled, her face crinkling into a beacon of happiness. Boone's own face lit with unfiltered joy. He picked her up and swung her in a circle. Neither could contain the laughter that bubbled within them and spilled out to the crowd, who cheered and clanked cups in toasts. The atmosphere was electric with excitement, elation. It was unforgettable—one of the best moments of my life.

Ewan was caught up in the moment, too, and pulled me into him. I looked up in wonder. My heart felt so full, so happy, so…

Could this be what it feels like to fall in love? I thought.

Since the loss of my mother, for the first time in my life good things had begun stacking on top of one another. I had found the place I belonged, I'd made beloved friends, I had family—two sets.

Gaspare had arranged for me to have Timbra back at The Root; Timbra's father had ceded his familial heritage to his political future. And it was beginning to feel possible to return the feelings Ewan had for me, which were much stronger than he had ever let on. My fractured heart had been re-glazed with love, acceptance, and potential. For a moment I thought my heart might shatter again, only this time, the thousand pieces would shoot up to meet the stars.

Pia's incessant buzzing brought me back to solid ground. I excused myself to check her message.

"Whattup, Pia?" I asked, unfettered by the distraction.

"You've received a message from S.D."

My heart plunged into my stomach. "Ah. Okay. What's it say? Please read it."

"Stella," Pia intoned. "Heard you're having a party. Sounds like fun. Came as far as the woods. Would love to join you."

What the hell is he thinking? He really is mad. "That's the entire message, Pia?"

"It is."

I had no idea what to do and ran a hand through my hair, which had been styled to perfection.

Timbra caught sight of my snafu. "I didn't spend twenty minutes on that wild red mess you call hair to have you pawing at it all night."

"Sorry," I jerked my hand from my head, but couldn't keep still.

"And now you're gnawing your cuticles. What's up with you? Is it Ewan?"

"No, no. It's nothing. Don't worry about it. This is your night. Let's go talk to Layla."

"Something's up with you, Stonewall. What is it?"

I let out a hard breath. I didn't want to tell her. Didn't want to acknowledge what was actually happening. She tapped a foot impatiently and stared me down.

"That guy from the bistro the other day?" She nodded in recognition. "He's here. Wants to come to the party."

"Great. The more the merrier."

"You don't understand. He's…he's. Well, there are still some things I've not yet told you about my family."

"Oh, for gods' sake, Stella. Just go get the guy. Tonight's a celebration. You know I don't have any hangups about your family."

"But. No. He's—"

"Go," she said, her voice deepening with force. "It's my party. Go get him, or I will."

I left, but resolved to talk Stryde out of joining the party. He didn't know anyone, after all. And he should definitely not be seen by so many people. It was my job to talk some sense into him.

What I didn't realize was how difficult it would be to talk sense into someone who'd lost his mind.

"Stryde, hello." He looked less agitated than he had before. There were no tremors that I noticed. His movements were smoother, less jerky. I breathed a little easier.

Stryde rushed me with a hug before I could step away from it. I stiffened at the awkward embrace, but endured it. At first. When he clutched me tighter and sniffed me, I wriggled for release. He didn't let go and my heart stuttered in panic. After pushing against his chest, he finally released me, though his gaze remained fixed on mine.

"You smell of wolf," he said. "Too much of wolf."

"You know what, Stryde? That is not your business. And I am awful damn tired of everybody sniffing me all the time. I don't care if it's a Thayerian thing, or that you can't help it. It's rude. Keep your nose to yourself."

"Is it the wolf's house? The party?"

"What? Yes. What are you doing here?"

He shrugged. "I came to see you. I want to meet your friends." He said it as though it was the most normal thing in the world.

"But, you can't. You're in hiding. If anyone recognizes you we're in big trouble."

"No one will recognize me. No one knows me. I've been away for a long time. Too long. I was cooped up with only my dad and grandma for years. And now I'm stuck in a minuscule cabin with them. I can't go anywhere, can't make new friends. Can't have people to my own home. Nothing's changed since our imprisonment. I'm going mad." He laughed without humor. "Well, *madder*. Please, Stella. I need this. I need to feel normal. To remember what it's like to be young again. To be free, if only for an hour."

My eyes fell closed and I shook my head. "It's not a good idea. There's just too much at risk. Things'll get better with time, Stryde. I know they will."

"Please," he whispered. His hopeless desperation was so evident it hurt my heart. My resolve turned to dust and floated to the forest floor.

"All right," I said. "But please, keep it together. This is a celebration. Enjoy yourself, and then go back to the safety of your cabin."

He smiled, and it almost didn't give me the creeps. He was truly happy. I knew he deserved happiness, and it was gratifying to know I could give him a little.

I held out my arm for a connection to trace together. Rather than hold my forearm, as intended, he ran his calloused fingers through my closed fist, forcing it open. He squeezed his fingers between mine in an odd, stiff clasp. I shook my head, gritted my teeth, and lifted a foot to take us back to the party.

When we arrived back near the pool Timbra noticed at once and waved a friendly hello to Stryde, who bowed formally in response. Ewan saw us, too, and made his way toward me.

"I don't think we've met," he said to Stryde and offered an outstretched hand.

When Stryde moved to return the greeting Ewan caught his scent. It was evident in his stiff posture, in the hard set of his jaw the moment he pieced it all together. His eyes shot to me, to Stryde, back to me. I could almost see the inner workings of his too-clever mind. He was running over the potential scenarios. I could almost imagine his thought process: should he throw Stryde out? Should he berate me for my stupidity in bringing him here? Should he alert the authorities? Should he keep cool, act like nothing was wrong, hope for the best, and let the celebration continue?

He must've chosen the latter.

When Stryde extended his hand, Ewan shook it stiffly, his jaws trembling under the weight of their pressure.

"I'm Stryde," my cousin said. "You must be the wolf. Thank you for your hospitality."

Ewan took a deep breath. He tried and failed to find words, and nodded instead. We all stood awkwardly for several long moments. It was a close contest of who was the most uncomfortable, but I thought it was probably me.

"Stella, may I speak with you for a moment?" Ewan finally said.

I followed him to the side of the house. "What the hell were you thinking?" he gritted the moment we rounded the log structure. My eyes shot toward the party; I hoped we were out of earshot. The way Thayerians could hear, though, probably not.

"He just showed up," I defended, my shoulders ascending to my ears. "He begged to come. Promised to be good. I…I felt sorry for him. He just wants to feel normal for a little while."

Ewan said nothing. He held his head in his hands, rubbed his eyes. "Well," he said after a beat and looked up. "There's nothing to be done about it now. Might as well go back."

He kissed me softly, reverently, and pulled back to catch my gaze. "Let's go join the celebration."

We found Stryde at the outdoor bar on his second shot of whiskey. *That's not good*, I thought. I pasted on a grin for Ewan and left him to make sure Stryde didn't get out of control.

"Better save some for everyone else," I said in a playful tone.

"Oh," Stryde replied. "Don't worry; I brought more." He produced a half-empty bottle from the back pocket of his pants. His fine black hair fell over one eye as he looked down at me blearily.

"Did you drink the other half of that?"

Stryde nodded pleasantly.

"Tonight? Before you came here?"

"Helps calm my nerves," he said before pressing the bottle to his lips. "Stops the tremors."

"I see. Maybe you'd better cool it for a little while? Keep your wits about ya?"

"You know what I'd really like?" he asked.

"What's that?" *Please say to go home. Please say to go home.*

"To dance."

I forced a laugh. "They're good, right? That's my friend Layla. Band's called Shiny Things. Go for it. They cleared a spot for a dance floor and everything."

"No," he said with a frown. "I want to dansh with you." *Did he just slur 'dance?'*

"Oh, I'd better not, Stryde. But thank you."

"Dance with me," he said and reached for my hands. I pulled them back just in time.

"I'd better go check on Timbra." I turned to find her, but he was in front of me before I could blink.

"Just one dance. I came all this way."

He wouldn't be deterred, and I decided to make the best of the situation. Maybe he'd be satisfied and move on. "Sure," I said tightly and followed him to the dance floor.

Shiny Things was in the middle of an up-tempo song. *Thank goodness,* I thought. *Slow dancing would be awkward.* But instead of dancing according to the music's tempo he grabbed me, holding my hand and clasping my waist so tightly I squirmed uncomfortably.

"Let me go, Stryde," I said, still holding out hope he'd listen to reason. Instead, he held me tighter, forcing my arms, my body to move with his like a string puppet. He danced us around the patio in stiff, jerky movements and the other guests eyed us warily.

I caught Layla's gaze as we passed her and put every bit of pleading I could into my eyes.

She tried to help. Her efforts were just misguided. She stopped the band mid-song and switched gears, slowing the music down. A ballad.

Relax, I told myself and willed toward Stryde. *Relax*. He slowed, and his grip on my hands loosened enough that the blood could reach my fingertips. I forced myself to breathe, to clear my head and find a peaceable way out of the situation.

The weight of Stryde's stare caused me to look up. He was too close. There was only room for the rank scent of whiskey between us. I wrenched back, but my neck could only extend so far. Stryde followed my head, his eyes intent on mine before he closed them. My stomach lurched with the realization he intended to kiss me.

"Stryde, no!" I jerked to free myself from him, but he returned his grip on my hands. "What are you doing?" I rasped. Keeping my voice down was a losing battle.

"I'm trying to kiss you," he said, his wide brow tight with the stirrings of indignation and rejection.

"Why the hell would you do *that*?"

He shook his head dumbly. "I got no response to the flowers I sent, nor the candy. I tried to take you to dinner but you left." He gave an unattractive grunt. "But you seem to be a woman of action. I'm hoping you'll respond to me physically."

His words, the rationale was so shocking, so bewildering, that my breaths came out in soft pants. Eventually I found the words I'd been searching for. "That was you? But…why? We just went through this whole incest thing with Brandubh. Why in the world would you ever think it was okay to pursue me?"

"Brandubh may be an evil bastard, but he's right about one thing: you're the only one there is for me, Stella. I knew it that the night in the crater. We're the last. Don't you see?" He squeezed my hands so tightly my bones ground together. "We must be together because we're the only ones."

I wriggled my fingers to regain some feeling in them, but I had bigger problems than my blood flow. "Let's…let's talk about this tomorrow," I said. "Okay? You sleep this off and we'll get Granny and Uncle Eiven's input. We'll work it out. You can find someone—find happiness again."

He'd heard nothing I said. And despite his heavy consumption of whiskey, his tremors had returned. He'd worked himself into a frenzy. "And when I learned you were an omni, I thought nothing could be more perfect. We'll never be at risk again. We can make offspring that have a defense against Brandubh. Just think, Stella. Because of your heritage, our kind can finally be free."

I looked around wildly for help, but who could solve this particular problem? No one but me.

"The only reason I got away from Brandubh that day was because he didn't expect me to be an omni. Now that he knows, it's no longer a defense. It was the surprise that gave me the upper hand. You see that, don't you?"

But he didn't see. Whether it was the booze or his addled brain, it didn't matter. He was beyond reason.

"Let her go, please," Ewan said from behind Stryde. Ewan's voice was laced with angry authority.

"You." Stryde released me to face Ewan, quick as a train of thought. His eyes hardened to determined green orbs, and I knew his fragile facade had cracked. "You've turned her against me. You think I don't know you're courting her, too?" Stryde scoffed. "I thought she'd be too smart to accept you, but I was wrong." A vicious snarl escaped his lips, and he shook himself, working hard to get back under control.

"Listen, man," Ewan said. "There's no competition here. You've got the wrong idea. Stella's not interested in you. I'm afraid I'm going to have to ask you to leave now."

I tried to stop Ewan mid-sentence, even though he'd kept his cool. He'd been as polite as possible under the circumstances. But there was no stopping Stryde's downward spiral. With each of Ewan's words, Stryde's vellum-thin psyche deteriorated further and further. His crazed eyes shot from side to side like emerald pinballs. His body vibrated with tremors and he sucked each breath like a dying man. He was going to break at any moment.

When he began to slaver onto his dress shirt as his mouth elongated and formed unnatural angles I knew the worst was about to happen. "Oh, damn," I breathed. "Damn, damn, damn."

The party goers began to comprehend that something was happening around them, and their worried conversations mingled to make a nervous soundtrack to the two men's impending fight.

Facing a physical threat, Ewan began to change, too. His face, which I'd always thought was a window to his kind soul, took on a look of evil menace. In the time it took to swallow the nervous lump in my throat, Ewan had transformed into a medieval wolf monster as huge as it was frightening.

Ewan's wolf form was gigantic and dangerous, but still no match for a dragon. He could never win a fight against Stryde. One strike, one bite, one fiery breath, and Ewan would be lost. That was unacceptable to me.

Though there were only milliseconds to consider them, I was aware of the repercussions of the action I was about to take. Once the crowd of people saw me go dragon they'd know. They'd soon know about the the Drakontos, and they'd soon know about me.

Conceal my true nature or protect Ewan Bristol?
It was the easiest decision I ever made.

28

Stryde Drakontos burst into his onyx dragon with a vicious roar heard for miles. The chattering crowd went silent as death, mouths agape at the unfathomable sight before them. The jerky movements of his body expanding and his gnarled black wings unfolding to their full length sent iron furniture skidding across the stamped concrete.

The crowd had dispersed in the few seconds it took for Stryde to change, but a nosey few poked their heads around corners and from under patio tables, too enthralled at the sight of a dragon to run completely to safety.

Stryde lifted his great head and shot a column of fire straight into the moonlight. It was for show, to intimidate, and it had the intended effect. Someone screamed in terror from just inside the cabin's back doors.

At Stryde's display, Ewan made one of his own, loosening a blood curdling string of growls and snarls. The two faced off in a metaphysical pissing contest.

I didn't have a penis, but I had power. I zeroed in on the center of my magical core, fanning the scorching flame of my chakra until I felt that familiar source of power just waiting to be tapped. I thought *release*, and surged into my auburn dragon.

My long neck stretched as I assimilated to the fearsome form, and then I used my leathery wing to force Ewan behind me. Though he put up a good fight I moved him aside like an annoyance.

He would hate that, I knew. But he'd live.

Stryde arched his wide head, his onyx scales gleaming from the light of the fire pit. He tried to reach around me to Ewan, but I blocked him.

"*Hiding behind a woman?*" Stryde's sneer was clear despite his words being unspoken. "*Did all men lose their balls while I was imprisoned, or just you? Where I come from, men fight like men.*"

From the corner of my eye I saw Boone's massive dog moving stealthily behind Stryde.

Behind me Ewan roared his frustration, growled his fury. He wanted a chance at Stryde, but that wasn't going to happen. I wouldn't let Boone get hurt, either.

A sharp pain high up on my tail caused me to whip my head around. Ewan released his grip on me with a nasty snarl. That was all the distraction Stryde needed. He angled for Ewan and opened his wide mouth. I knew what came next. He'd burn Ewan alive.

Quick as a snake strike I dove for Stryde and held his wide neck between my deadly teeth. He couldn't expel fire held like that. He hissed, pulled to free himself, but couldn't break free of my grip. The blood my teeth had drawn as he struggled was hot on my tongue.

"*All right, Stryde,*" I taunted. "*Let's leave these lightweights out of it. You want me? You're gonna have to catch me.*" I exploded into the air, and he took the bait. Ewan, the fight, and the party were forgotten as he vaulted for me.

Ewan's furious howl resonated through the skies toward us before he sent through my mind, "*Dammit, Stella. No!*" But his voice faded and became imperceptible as I launched toward my beloved stars and away from my beloved friends.

Once in flight, reality kicked in. I was on my own against Stryde, who was bigger and a more experienced fighter and flyer. *Damn.* But speed was on my side, and employed that advantage. My plans had ended at getting Stryde away from Ewan and the group. *Where to now?* I thought.

An idea struck. Bay and Eiven had experience getting through to Stryde. Maybe they could help me get him through this psychotic break. With my knobbed feet tucked tightly into my chest, I speared for the Drakontos' hidden cabin.

The odd pressure on my brain as Stryde tried to communicate with me was familiar. I'd blocked his maddened rambling moments after taking off. But as we approached the hideout I opened myself up to alert Bay and Eiven and caught fragments of his frenzied thoughts again. "*Won't see it. Be together. Need more time. Away from those dogs. That school. Live here. Force her. Know all about that. Give in eventually.*"

"*Bay*!" I mentally shouted. "*Eiven! Help me. Stryde's lost his shit. He's chasing me. Help!*" I flew low against the cabin, chuffed my big wings over the top to rattle it, to get their attention.

"*Stella*?" Eiven sent up. "*What's wrong*?"

"*Need help now! Stryde. Psychotic break. Taken up Brandubh's idea to trap me, breed me.*"

"*What*?" Bay chimed in. "*No. That's ridiculous. Come down here, we'll work this all out.*"

They weren't moving nearly fast enough—didn't understand the seriousness of the situation.

"*Get your asses up here*!" I tried my best to relay the emergency, but yelling without sound, well, it's hard. "*He's out of his freaking mind. He tried to kill my boyfriend.*" Fire spewed from Stryde's angry mouth at my words. I felt the heat of it on my flank, just above one of my back legs. "*See! He's gonna kill me, too*!"

"*No. Mine. Deserve this. Need.*" Stryde's barely perceptible thoughts filtered down to Bay and Eiven, who had begun to grasp the situation.

"*I think she's right, Eiven,*" Bay said and her body convulsed with the tremors of the anticipated transformation.

"Stryde," Eiven bellowed to the tops of the trees, but Stryde heard no one. He was stuck inside his head, the setting of his fractured brain switched to achieve or annihilate.

I dove and flipped, ascended and spun as best I could in my effort to escape him. But he was an adept flyer, and caught me as I tried to double back toward the cabin. Though my scales were designed to withstand the heat of another dragon's flame, Stryde knew my weaknesses. He exploited them when he shot a scorching plume toward the softer scales behind my knees. My hind quarter exploded in excruciating pain and the force of my reaction shot me toppling over the evergreens below. Tough armor covered my body, but the hard trunks of the trees still knocked the breath from me.

Out-hrust wings helped stop my descent, and I slid roughly into a thick copse of trees. I was confused and shook my head to try to push some of the sense that had been dislodged back into the front of my mind. Everything was foggy and moving so slowly—it felt like a dream. But it wasn't a dream, and I had to think faster or be in real trouble.

In an attempt to rise from the forest floor, it was apparent my right leg was badly wounded. I limped and hopped awkwardly for a while, crashing into the trees around me. Finally, my big body relaxed onto a large oak.

Resting for a moment, I forced breaths in through my nose; out through my mouth. I aimed to center myself, to assess my next move, but was pulled from my planning by the sound of Stryde's screech as he flew in search of me.

Could I just hide here? I thought. *It would be impossible in this form, but I had others....*

My eyes fell closed as I searched for my chakra. It was more difficult in the dragon form; less natural. I had an impulse to rub my chest just over my heart, but my gnarled claws prevented that. Instead I welcomed the soothing sounds of the forest around me. A crow cawed a warning overhead and somewhere a mouse scurried under a tuft of leaves. My eyes flew open at the nearby sound of something scrambling away. A fox. A tiny red fox with big, pert ears and a narrow snout. Quick, small, clever. My lips pulled back from my vicious teeth in a smile I'm sure would scar small children for life.

My line of sight, the scents of the forest—everything changed so fast and made me dizzy. I'd gone from towering into the canopy of trees down to the underbrush and leaves below them in a matter of seconds. My narrow tongue thrust out on a pant while I recovered.

My sly grin came naturally, for I'd mimicked the form of the little red fox.

Break time was over, and I shot out in the direction of the Drakontos' cabin. It was urgent that I explain to Bay and Eiven the extent of Stryde's dementia. My little body extended almost horizontally between long, quick gallops.

They were standing in the small clearing outside the house watching Stryde circle overhead. Looking for me. I approached the house but didn't slow down. Instead I skidded right past them into the cover of the small cabin.

An old bath robe I'd found in one of the bedrooms served as a cover once I'd changed back to myself. Bay and Eiven had both seen me, and soon followed me inside.

I wasn't sure how the whole telepathy thing worked or how far the channels extended. But in my human form, at least I could whisper. "Can he hear us?" I asked softly.

"No, but what the hell's going on?" Eiven boomed.

Bay squeezed his thick arm with aged, knobby hands. "Shhh," she said sharply before turning to me. "What the hell is going on?"

"Stryde's lost his damn mind, that's what. I don't have time to get into all of it, but he thinks I've spurned him. He's been…courting me."

"Why the hell did you let him do that?" Bay yelped, her top lip rising toward her nose with each word.

I threw my head back in exasperation. "I didn't know," I seethed. "He was sending me flowers, candy, coming to see me. I thought the gifts were from someone else. That he just wanted to get to know me. I had no idea he saw himself as my…suitor. Jesus." I scrubbed at my eyes with the palms of my hands. "Now he's furious with both me and the guy I'm actually with—"

"Rowan Gresham," Eiven gave a disapproving nod.

I sucked a breath in through my teeth. "Well. No. Ewan Bristol."

"I thought you were seeing Mr. Gresham," Bay said.

"I was. Now it's Ewan."

The two exchanged a look.

"Oh, please," I said. "None of this is any of your business. But what *is* your business is that psychotic asshole circling the skies so he can find and steal me."

"He wouldn't harm you. He's just confused. He has a har—"

"He has a harder time with all of this than you, I know. But it's worse than you think. He's already tried to kill me and Ewan. He's got his mind set on this. He thinks because my father was an omni we can produce a breed of dragons not susceptible to Brandubh or something. I'm telling you, he thinks to keep me here, that I'll eventually see things his way."

"He's no' wrong," mused Bay.

"What?" I yelled before catching myself and saying more quietly, "You can't be serious."

"No, no. I only meant about you. He's no' wrong. You seem to be impervious to Brandubh."

"Okay, neither of you seems to be taking me seriously." The too-big sleeves of my borrowed robe flapped wildly as I waved my arms in distress.

"I'll go talk to him," Eiven said. "Try to calm him d—" Stryde's massive wings knocked dust from the cabin's rafters as he thundered overhead. He screamed in frustration. He knew I was inside.

Without another word he shot a column of fire down the cabin's ancient chimney, sending chunks of mortar, charred wood, and a cloud of ash throughout the house. I coughed and sputtered while attempting to rub the dirt from my stinging eyes. But those minor concerns were soon forgotten. Stryde sent another plume through the house, and the fire made it through.

A blanket thrown over the back of an old chair ignited, which caught to the chair itself. In mere seconds, flaming pieces of fabric fell onto the rug, causing it, too, to erupt in flame. Bay grabbed wildly for blankets and water as flames licked everything in their path.

Eiven's typically docile demeanor was gone. In its place was a terrifying mask of rage. His big body began to thrum with anger, with power. I scampered away from him and lost my footing, but he never noticed me. He was intent on the dragon demolishing his his home and threatening Bay and me.

Eiven shook a finger at his son. "Stryde Drakontos," he roared to the skies and stepped onto the small front porch. "Get control of yourself."

I huddled in the bedroom behind a wall. I had nowhere to go and sat rapt on the scene unfolding in front of me. Bay had managed to douse the last of the flames and stood, heaving, just inside the door.

"*You think you can control me, too*," Stryde hissed through our brains. He circled one last time before landing on the ground with a thud that rocked the cabin.

"Someone needs to," said Eiven. "You've set our cabin on fire. You've scared this girl to death. Try to calm down, son. Just go gather yourself. Take a long flight, work through your frustrations. Come back when your head's back on straight."

"*My head is straight*," Stryde seethed. "*For the first time. I'm through being shit on. I'm done following orders. I'm doing things my way now. If you don't like it, get out of the way.*"

"Son, you're upset, and no one can blame you for that. But you're not thinking right. Go clear your head. Come back when you've calmed some."

"*You think I don't know what you've planned?*" Stryde flapped his mighty wings causing tiny dust tornadoes. "*You think I don't know you want her for yourself.*"

What the hell is wrong with these people, I thought. *Will this nonsense ever end?* For the most part, I'd found Thayer to be quite civilized considering its people descended from animals and still got furry on the regular. But these lunatics insisted on sniffing my butt, on peeing on me to mark their territory. And I was sick of it.

"Now, you've got the wrong idea, son," Eiven said gently. "And I'm sorry to tell you she doesn't see you like that."

At Eiven's words Stryde opened his wide mouth and screeched so loudly I covered my ears inside the house. The sound didn't just grate my nerves, but caused a visceral panic to rise within me. The scream was ear-splitting, like someone was being crucified.

The furious shriek went on so long I wondered what was happening outside to keep Stryde so enraged. I pulled my hands from my ears and discovered Bay was screaming, too. She wailed over and over, the only reprieve when she stopped to inhale a breath. Her cries were frantic, hysterical. I crawled on all fours to peek around the door, my knuckles white as I gripped the wooden trim.

What I saw stopped my heart's beating.

Eiven had fallen to his knees on the porch, the pain and the force of Stryde's deadly fire too much to withstand. I watched with wide, horror-stricken eyes as Eiven fell heavily over onto the ground.

Bay threw her head and shoulders back in anguish and sank to her own knees. Hot tears ran down her cheeks, leaving skin-colored streaks among the black she'd collected from fighting the house fire.

Bay continued to scream even as she began to change. Her granny-like features disappeared into hard edges moments before she burst through the roof of the tiny cabin, sending chunks of wood, pieces of the house flying into the forest. She shot toward Stryde with determined fury, but he evaded her. She pulled up hard and chased him into the sky, all the while releasing that mournful cry. In seconds, the two disappeared into the night sky.

I rushed from the house to Eiven's unmoving form. As I got closer, it was clear he was gone.

The substantial force of Stryde's fiery attack had decimated my sweet uncle. He lay in a charred black mass on the porch, his outline the only thing still distinguishable.

The smell of creosote, of death, caused bile to pool in the back of my throat and I gagged as sweat formed on my forehead and above my lip. My eyes watered and welled over; whether a physical or emotional response to the grotesque murder of my uncle, I didn't know.

The old gray robe provided some relief as I covered my nose and attempted to breathe through my mouth. My hands hung limply at my sides as I stood over what was left of Eiven, at a loss for what to do. In the end I did nothing but weep.

A noise in the distance pulled me back to the reality of the volatile situation. If Stryde could obliterate strong, sturdy Eiven, he'd have no problem with me. Resolved to escape, I ran through the woods. The forest was so dense with fallen trees and underbrush that I tripped on the over-sized robe twice in my haste. With raw knees and scraped arms I continued to run, finally making it far enough from the cabin to stop and catch my breath.

Where to go? Not back to Ewan and my friends. And I couldn't abandon Bay by tracing to the protective wards of The Root. I had to save her, to get her away from Stryde before he killed her, too. It was also essential his damage be mitigated by keeping him far away from people. The woods were the best place for that.

Beads of sweat rolled down my forehead into my eyebrows as I thought frantically, trying to form some kind of plan. When I pulled the sweat-soaked sleeve from my face my back tingled with awareness. Chill bumps began at my scalp and erupted all down the skin of my body. Someone was watching me.

Stryde was suspended silently in the air behind me like a maniacal avenging angel. My knees lost their ability to hold me upright, and I grasped a nearby tree for support.

"*There you are*," Stryde said pleasantly. Like he hadn't a care in the world. Like he hadn't just killed his own father in a berserk rage.

"Stryde, just let me go." My voice cracked as I pleaded, "Please."

"*Don't cry dear one*," he murmured through my mind. "*Everything'll work out fine. Don't you see? We can be together now.*"

Enraging him further was a deadly move, so I said nothing. My hands, my entire body began to shake. I closed my eyes in an attempt to compose myself. When I finally opened them again, from the corner of my eye I saw something small and brown rising from the tree line behind Stryde. I dared alert him to Bays approach, but instead worked to keep his attention on me.

"How can this work, Stryde? Tell me."

He began to ramble nonsensically, going on in partial and scattered thoughts about our fates together. He became agitated again and twitched almost rhythmically, but it had worked. Stryde had no idea Bay'd swooped in behind him.

As she neared several gaping tears in her large wings were visible, as were singed and raw places on her face and spiny back. Her battle with Stryde had been a tough one—for her.

Stryde's crazed eyes snapped to a squint when he realized my attention was somewhere behind him, and he flung his heavy neck around.

"*Thought I killed you, old woman,*" he seethed.

"*Stryde,*" Bay's voice was hollow. "*How can you be so pitiless? Your own father is dead. I'm the only family you have left, child.*"

Stryde blinked his reptilian eyes rapidly, like he'd been caught in the rain, then raised his wide neck and roared, "*I'm sick of the past. Sick of you, of what we call a life. Sick of hiding, of hurting. I deserve a future. And I'm going to make one.*"

After expelling those ominous words he made a deliberate inhale of deadly breath. He opened his hinged mouth to cauterize Bay, too.

I snapped.

The loss of my kind uncle had cut me deeply. I'd had enough of Stryde's attempts to manipulate me, of treating me like a damned incubator. While his attention was focused on Bay my dragon rippled to life. I welcomed her power, her speed, her defensive armor. I embraced the sharp tremors that resulted in leashing her need for vengeance.

Stryde's head swung in my direction with a measured drawl. His wild eyes betrayed no fear in facing two dragons. Only anticipation of the fight, the violence. He was lost; I knew that. But Bay tried one last time to lure him from the jungle of madness he'd wandered into long ago.

"*Stryde,*" she said gently. "*It's time to go home, child. Enough—*"

Stryde's abdomen expanded on another inhale, his great onyx scales glinting in the moonlight.

Without further thought, I roared my fear, my rage, and something inside me cracked. The imaginary fissure that had formed that day in the clearing gaped to expose the entire well of my fire. The magical missile flew from my open mouth with a force so powerful I braced myself to stay upright.

I hadn't aimed well—hadn't truly expected for my flame to ignite. But it had, and had set fire to a small stand of trees. The flame missed Stryde completely and only succeeded in pissing him off.

When he thrust his powerful back legs and wings to vault toward me, I knew I was dead.

I always heard that your life flashes before your eyes in the moments before death, but that's not what happened to me.

The experiences I'd never had called to me like a tragically lost lover from beyond the grave. I yearned for them, lamented the unfairness of losing my life so early in the game—of being snatched away when I was just beginning to scratch the surface of who I was. I loathed Stryde for taking them from me, for snuffing my life so soon. I vowed to return and haunt his demented ass until I drove him completely over the edge.

The morbid, angry thoughts flashed in the infinitesimal time before Stryde bit down on my armored throat. He aimed for my body, too, and the sting of his sharp talons as they penetrated even the tough scales of my side was excruciating. My esophagus constricted beneath his mighty jaws and I saw only blinding white just before my vision went black.

Stryde's grip on my throat had slackened as he opened his mouth in a gasp. I was completely freed when he threw his head back and shrieked in agony. Full mental function hadn't resurfaced, but I didn't wait to ask questions and scrambled quickly away.

He was…smoking. He looked to be on fire from the inside out. His long neck thrashed wildly and he clawed at the soft ground, sending chunks of mud and debris through the trees. His crazed eyes were wide with shock, with pain, and—finally—with fear.

Then they held no emotion at all. Stryde's jade eyes closed just before his big body fell to the forest floor with a thud that shook the trees around us. He didn't rise again.

"*Bay,*" I called and rushed toward her. "*You're hurt.*" She was bleeding in several places, her wings as singed and holey as melted canvas.

"*I'll be all right, dear,*" she said, but her eyes had lost the light behind them. They were flat. A million miles away.

"*Is—is he…dead?*" His body betrayed no real wounds. He wasn't bleeding; nothing appeared broken. I'd seen him smoking, but it was far different than the death Eiven had faced.

"*Aye,*" she said, her gaze still distant. "*I tried everythin' I knew. Broken as he was, I loved him still. Poor dear. He didn't know* how *to pursue happiness.*" Her head hung sadly. "*When he came for you—after what he did to my Eiven—*"

Bay closed her eyes as pain twisted her features. She came close to breaking down, but never did. After a moment she went on, "*I knew he'd kill you, too.*" I took no pleasure in nodding my agreement.

"*But, are you sure he's gone? He's not burned. I didn't see you bite or fight him. What did you do?*"

"*Tis called the fire within. It's magic as ancient and evil as we dragons. It's the nucleus of our own fire called up by a spell. Few have ever manipulated it; even Stryde did not know it. Fewer still ever will, for the dragons are no more.*"

"*That's some wicked shit,*" I thought.

Bay swung her burdened eyes at me and nodded. "*Aye. I'd hoped to never use it again.*"

"*I—I'm sorry. I know you loved him. I'm sorry for your loss. Sorry you had to do that.*"

"*I'm so tired,*" she said. "*I'd just like to go home and rest.*" At my shifty eyes and pained expression she remembered what waited for us at the cabin. She heaved a ragged breath and closed her eyes. "*Will ye help me bury them, dear?*"

"Of course. I'll carry Stryde, too. You can change back. Try to heal."

Bay found a large scrap of the robe I'd worn and attempted to cover herself with it.

Stryde's body had begun to cool, and had reverted to his human form. His face was so peaceful in death one would never suspect the trauma he'd just endured or the madness he'd displayed moments before. His sleek black hair lay scattered over the side of his slack face.

I clasped his limp body as gently as I could with my back legs and extended my wings in flight, carrying him along the tops of the trees toward the cabin hideaway.

29

At the sight of my uncle Eiven's incinerated body my grip tightened on Stryde. Being angry would do no good now, but I couldn't help the feeling. Such a tragic, stupid loss—untimely and premature. And now the family I was so happy to discover, that I had such high hopes for, was reduced to only one: my granny, Bay.

She'd be alone now in this reclusive hideaway. Alone with her grief. No one could be expected to deal with that loss, on top of everything else she'd endured, and come out normal on the other side. I wasn't sure what I could do to help, but was committed to finding some way to comfort her.

The task at hand, though, was laying my uncle and his son to rest.

There was an area large enough just west of the cabin, and I lay Stryde down there.

Withering into my normal self, I stretched my aching back and arms. My body was tight from the overwhelming stress of the night.

Inside the house was one of my uncle's old shirts, a pair of shorts, and work boots. A nearby storage shed held shovels, and I drug them to the burial site.

Bay ambled into the clearing as I stood over Stryde attempting to estimate how big the hole should to be. *Could Bay and I even dig a grave*? I thought. Shoveling was tough work. I knew from the days of gardening with my mother.

My mother. She would want to know her brother had died. Hell, she'd want to know that her own mother still lived. But I couldn't tell her. There'd been no word from her in the weeks since she'd left.

But while the scars I had from her abandonment were still tender and pink, they were healing, and I didn't cry when I touched them anymore. I hoped she'd found some peace. I hoped she'd been able to work through her issues. I hoped she'd come to the conclusion that she was wrong to leave, and come back. None of this seemed likely, but an eternal optimist can hardly just stop hoping.

"You picked a fine spot, dear," Bay called, pulling me from my reverie. Her voice was hollow, perfunctory as she sank onto one of the log-hewn seats around the fire pit. She seemed unfathomably old at that moment. And tired. Her shoulders hunched so far that her neck disappeared into her body. She sat unmoving and I didn't disturb her. Instead I supported myself on the handle of the shovel and relived the few memories I had of Eiven, and even of Stryde. Bay was likely doing the same.

With obvious effort she finally stirred and limped toward the cabin, reemerging in her own clothes.

"I don't know how—do I just start digging? I've never done this before."

"Aye, I've experience enough for us both," she said. "One shovel of earth at a time, dear. That's how you do it."

And so we dug. Bay's weary body was resilient, determined. Together we carved a small, deep hole.

"That'll do," she said.

"But, it's not nearly big enough. I can keep going if you're tired."

"I'm tired, it's true. But Stryde is already starting to wither away, and Eiven—"

Bay's voice broke and she fell to her knees. I didn't rush to her; leaning on someone for support wasn't her style. I looked away and let her grieve in as much privacy as I could offer.

She finally let go. She wailed and gnashed at her hair and neck. She bent to the ground and beat her fists into the rich, black earth until she could move them no more.

Eventually she dragged herself back up, and her arms hung loosely at her sides as she knelt in the dirt. She turned her face skyward leaving her misery open to the heavens.

"Eiv—" Bay cleared her hoarse throat. "We'll have to gather Eiven's remains and bring them. We can sprinkle them over Stryde. He'd like that."

At the reminder I glanced at Stryde's body, but couldn't make sense of what I saw. He had reduced to a dense lump, his body turning in and shrinking like melted plastic. Bay'd been right. He would fit in the hole.

She gathered Stryde gingerly and placed him in the grave, then closed her eyes in silent goodbye. I followed her to the porch for Eiven.

"Will ye get the smaller tarp from the shed, dear?" Bay asked.

I soon discovered the need for the tarp, for once we disturbed Eiven's remains they crumbled to dust and small, dry chunks. Together Bay and I slid the flat canvas under Eiven's charred remains in an effort to salvage them for transport. The process took a long time, though the task itself wasn't labor intensive. Each time we began, Bay would stop for several hard moments and breathe in an effort to regain her composure. She had difficulty looking at the black mass, but dealt with the task at hand as she did most things: with utilitarian, purpose-driven efficiency. I envied Bay's ability to remove emotion from necessity. But I didn't envy the countless heartaches and trials she'd endured in order to develop the ability.

I felt her pain, her sorrow—along with some of my own—and my emotions manifested with force as I worked, though she never said a word.

We folded Eiven's remains into the tarp like a flag ceremony at a soldier's funeral. She held them reverently to her chest and carried them to the grave site before unfolding them onto Stryde's shriveled body. We both stared into the grave unmoving, not speaking.

My legs gave out with exhaustion, but I caught myself before I fell down completely. Bay sought my gaze, but remained stony.

"What now?" I whispered.

"Now we replace the soil, dear."

At the thought of moving earth, a scratchy vision began to play behind my eyes. It was something I'd seen Gaspare do. Something I never dreamed I'd do myself. In the premonition I used a magic I didn't know I possessed to cover the grave with a wave of my hand. The vision then expanded to reveal Bay's reaction to my magic, and her acceptance of it. She lay her eyes closed and nodded a weary encouragement.

The premonition gave me the confidence, the permission I needed, and I returned the heavy soil to the hollow, closing the grave of Eiven and Stryde Drakontos.

She didn't address what I'd done, but said, "You're tired, girl. Will ye stay here?"

I suspected she asked as much for herself as she did for me. "Yes," I said. "Thank you."

A groan left my aching throat as I approached consciousness. It was less a result of the awkward position I woke in than the sore muscles from the night before. Hastily changing into several forms, a fight for my life, the digging of a grave—all events I'd rather not be reminded of, but my aching body had different ideas.

Bay was in the kitchen, a kettle of coffee over an open flame in the old stove top. She sensed my awareness but didn't look at me. "Coffee and bacon's on the stove," she said. "Be done in a jif."

I nodded and pried myself from the couch.

"I'll be leavin' after we eat," she said.

"What?" I croaked and looked up. "Where're you goin?"

She finished drying her hands and lay the worn dish towel on the counter. She'd pulled her gray hair back into a bun—practically the only granny-like thing about her. She dragged her dull green eyes in my direction and combed her hair back nervously with her fingers.

"I'm goin' to find yer mam," she said. "Goin' to yer world."

"My world—why? What do you mean?"

"I canna stay here," she said firmly. "There's nae reason." Her accent was thick—whether from emotions or exhaustion, I didn't know. "With Eiven and Stryde gone, I've nothin'. I willna stay here alone."

"But," I stuttered. "I'll stay here with you. I won't leave you alone, Bay."

"Nae, dear. Ye canna be seen with me, and ye know it well."

"No one will know," I argued. "I'll go to school each day and return in the afternoons. I'll think of some excuse."

"No. I willna have ye sacrificin' for me. My mind's made. You and Edina are all I have left. I know yer safe at The Root, where ye belong. But I dinna know where my Edina is."

Her eyes softened and her speech slowed. "I'll find her, help her remember who she is. I'll bring her back."

I stepped toward Bay and reached to run my hands around her shoulders. I'd never tried to hug her before—nor she me. But I held her to me like I'd lose her, too. She exhaled a weary breath and squeezed me back.

"You don't know where to look," I said as I held her. "Let me go with you."

"No, dear," she said, in control of emotions once more. "I'll go. I didna make it this long without a good head on my shoulders, and a few tricks up my sleeve. I'll be fine. And it'll be best if I find her alone."

She was right, but it still seemed so sudden, such a rash decision after the horrific loss she'd suffered.

Though a change of scenery might be best.

"Okay," I said. "Okay. And when you find her…tell her…tell her I miss her. That I'm fine; I'll make it, but I miss *her*."

Bay looked up at me, and the wrinkles of her face had doubled overnight. They carved deep lines across her forehead, around her tired eyes and down sunken cheeks.

She nodded her gray head and wiped a single tear from my eye with the pad of her thumb.

30

I stayed at the cabin with Bay until she left. She recovered from her lapse of emotion and gathered her things almost clinically. She nodded goodbye to me, promised she'd see me again, and traced away.

Once she was gone, I wasn't sure what to do with myself. Emotionally and physically hung-over, home was my most pressing need, so I traced to the end of my bed in Sabre Hall. I fell backward onto my soft quilt, allowing the comfort and familiarity of my bed to embrace me for a glorious moment.

"*Whatthehellareyoudoinghere?*" whispered Timbra through my mind. "*Are you insane? You can't be here.*"

"Wha—" I began and she shushed me with authority.

"*Hush. Don't make a sound. They're monitoring your room. They'll know you're here.*"

"*Who's monitoring my room?*" I shot back. "*And why?*"

"*Why? You can't be serious. You turned into your freaking dragon in front of half The Root. Thank the gods you put that ward around your room or they'd have caught you when you traced in. Ha! They were so furious when they couldn't enter. Tried everything they knew. And you owe Emrynne big time. She stood there and watched the entire thing. Never offered to take down the ward; she never told them it was hers.*"

"*Slow down!*" I yelled to the best of my telepathic ability. "*Who tried everything they new? Who's after me?*"

"The damned authorities, Stella. Radix Admin. Gresham. Everyone. Why you came back here is beyond me. You have to leave. Now."

"Leave? But. I don't have anywhere to go. Maybe I can just explain. A lot's happened. The dragons are all gone."

"What do you mean, 'gone?' Wait. Never mind. You've got to get out of here. We can talk later."

I groaned pitifully and tried to collect my thoughts. Where could I go?

Not to Ewan's—that was the last place I'd been seen. *Oh no.* I hoped we didn't destroy too much of his beautiful family home. And I hoped his family wasn't suspect or being interrogated. *Oh god.* Memories of how I'd shoved him behind me, thrown him from Stryde's reach, came flooding back. He was probably furious with me. But he was alive; he could be mad just as long as he needed—he was still breathing.

Gresham's was out. Who could I trust. Layla's mother? No. That would just be dragging someone else into my mess.

Gaspare? I felt close to him, connected. I knew he cared for me, too. But his political responsibilities made how he'd respond to my predicament an unknown. I had enough 'unknowns' to deal with and couldn't risk another.

Finally the obvious trickled to the front of my muddy brain.

"I'm going somewhere safe," I sent to Timbra in her room. *"I'm not telling you where, just in case. But meet me at sundown where we skinny-dipped after the Solstice Fest. I'll tell you everything."*

"Okay," she said. *"Be safe, girl."*

"I'll do my best."

The Drakontos' cabin was lonely without them. Too quiet, with too many ghosts. I wasn't frightened of being there, and it was still daylight out, but Eiven and Stryde's fresh graves were just feet away. If I'd had anywhere else in the world to go, I would have. Choosing to be alone was one thing. But being relegated to a hideout without human contact at the same location I'd just dug a grave for two dead relatives was another thing entirely.

If I'd been using my brain, I would've forced Bay to let me go with her. I'd been so distraught about Eiven and Stryde, about her own departure, that I didn't think back to the party the night before. I never once considered what had happened after I left Ewan's to lure Stryde from the guests; from him.

Of course everyone knew about me now. We'd invited fifty people. No way could you mitigate that kind of damage.

I ran my hands over my gritty face, scrubbed at my eyes. Time was irrelevant, nonexistent, and I stared at nothing pulling strands of my auburn hair through my fingers over and over.

I read once that in stressful situations, the higher up on one's body their hands were placed, the worse the situation and the feeling of hopelessness. This was a doozy.

What I really needed was a shower. That struck me as a helluva great idea. It was also the only idea I had.

The primitive cabin had less what I'd call a shower, and more what I'd call a trickle. But it was water, there was soap, and I lost myself in the mindless effort to scrub my body clean. I emerged no less at a loss of what to do, but at least less foul. And that was something. Baby steps away from bleakness.

I busied myself throughout the day with chores. First, I tackled the gaping hole in the roof of the cabin left by Bay's furious exit. I used the remaining tarp to cover the hole and tied it down as best I could.

Next was cleaning up the musty retreat. I couldn't find the willpower to remove Eiven and Stryde's belongings from their room, but did move Bay's things in with them. If this was to be my home for a while, I might as well have my own space. Maybe Timbra could sneak the rest of my clothes out; I'd only grabbed a few essentials when I rushed from Sabre.

One of the few small windows revealed twilight approaching. I changed, pulled my hair back, and left to meet Timbra at the swimming hole near the Basel River where we'd been so wild, so carefree, just a few weeks before.

Tracing just beyond the sandy bank, I waited at the tree line. There was no way to know if she would come alone, as planned. Nervous and edgy, I jumped at every stray sound.

I waited. Waited. I mindlessly traced circles in the dirt with my sneaker when rustling near the water alerted me to someone's presence. Timbra's cervid ancestry gave her the ability to move eerily quietly, so the noise level frightened me. I backed deeper into the woods and squatted behind a fallen tree trunk.

Then I caught scent of him. Ewan. Sweet, strong…home. I ran from my hiding spot right into his waiting arms. He buried his face in my shoulder, wrapped his big arms around me and squeezed so hard and so long I thought I'd meld into him.

He wrapped the long hair of my ponytail around his hand and pulled back to look me over.

I couldn't meet his gaze.

"Hey," he said softly. "Look at me."

"I was afraid you'd be furious with me," I said, my eyes still downcast.

"I am," he rasped, and I flinched. "I'm mad as hell."

He took my lips in his soft, warm ones, then leaned his forehead against mine. We stayed that way—his big hands in my hair, his forehead pressed to mine, his chest heaving with relieved breaths.

"I'm sorry," I said. "I had to save you, Ewan. Pushing you behind me was…emasculating, I know, but Stryde was crazy. He could take you out with one strike. I had to get him away from you, from everyone."

Ewan lifted his face and his chestnut eyes scorched my mine. I flinched at the depth of emotion they betrayed. He held my face in his hands and ran his thumbs across my cheekbones.

"I don't care about that," he said. "Where have you been? I was so afraid he hurt you. I didn't know where to look, but I searched all night." His breath left his chest in a shudder. "I was afraid you wouldn't come back."

I lay my head on his firm shoulder, and tears threatened to spill onto my cheeks. I wiped my eyes on his heathered shirt and squeezed his tight middle.

"Don't ever do that to me again, Stella." He shook me, just a little, and I swallowed hard. Couldn't yet speak. "I can't take it," he went on. "I can't lose you. I won't."

Ewan's curly hair was wild from his long night searching for me. I touched his lips with my fingertips, recalling the feel of them that night at the lake, the perfection we had achieved. I thought about how afraid I'd been for his life, how easily the sacrifice of revealing my dragon came when compared to losing him.

Then I remembered the vicious look in Ewan's eyes as he closed his slavering wolf mouth on the scales of my tail.

"You bit my ass," I accused.

"Mmm," he agreed, then his smile turned wicked. "And I'll do it again if you're good."

I laughed and snuggled tightly into his big body.

The conspicuous clearing of a man's throat pulled me back to the present. My gaze shot to the direction of the sound—to the river bank—and there in the dark I saw the outlines of Boone, Timbra, Layla, and Mari.

"But... What are you all doing here?" I asked and stepped away from Ewan.

"We wanted to come. We want to help—however we can." Boone's deep voice held authority, finality.

"No. You can't be here. If they find out you're associating with me you'll all be in trouble, too."

"We're willing to take that risk," Layla said. "We know what you are—who you are. And we accept that."

"But…you hate dragons. Everyone does. And for good reason. If you think you accept who I am then you don't know the whole story."

"They know the whole story." Timbra swung her doe eyes up to meet mine, and her ears twitched nervously. She was guilty but determined. She'd told them.

"What did you do?" I breathed.

"What did *I* do?" she squeaked. "*You* turned into a flippin' dragon in front of half the school. It was either tell the truth or let imaginations run wild. I chose the truth. I chose to defend you."

"She did the right thing, Stell," Ewan said. "We all support you; we know who you really are. Those of us here knew at least some of it already."

"And now everyone knows," I said and sat down in the sand. I held my head in my hands, covered my eyes and asked, "How bad is it?"

No one responded. I risked a look at each of their faces. Layla was tediously studying the back of her hand. Mari helped. Boone and Timbra looked at each other sideways and threw elbows as if to say *'You do it.' 'No, you do it.'*

Ewan's high cheeks fell when his smile disappeared. His face was no longer filled with relief, but with pity.

I hate pity—such a useless emotion. Hope, that's helpful. Fear is useful at least. But pity? No thank you.

"How bad, Ewan?" He moved his head from side to side, trying—and failing—to fool me with his aloof body language. "Give it to me straight. I can take it. This day can't possibly get any worse."

"Well," he stalled. "There aren't any formal charges or anything. But, ah, the school, the town, and in fact, the fair majority of Thayer is in an uproar about the revelation that dragons exist. They know you're one of them. I mean, you changed right there for all to see." When I began to protest he stopped me. "I know you had to. If left unchecked Stryde could have decimated the entire party. We told them that—that you defended me, all of us, and sacrificed yourself."

"The problem is," Boone said gently, "no one really differentiates between you and Stryde. A dragon's a dragon, in most views. There's no good or bad person, just a dragon, which people have feared and hated their whole lives."

Timbra nodded. "And the people who interviewed me asked how many more dragons were out there. They fear another attack; that there's a militia of surviving dragons planning to attack Thayer again."

"Oh, that's ridiculous," I scoffed. "I'm sorry I've dragged you into this mess. Who interviewed you? What did they say?"

"There was a committee from The Root," Timbra rolled her eyes. "Vice Chancellor Edgecliffe, Professor Lochlain…Dean Miles."

"Dean Mi—are you kidding me? She hates me already. Hell. I—"

"That's not all," Timbra cut in. "Government officials, too."

I squinted my eyes at her and she shrugged. It wasn't her fault, after all. "Anyone I know?" I knew the answer to that question.

"Gresham," she said.

Ewan growled low in his throat and stepped forward to loom over me. I looked up at him from my seat in the sand and gave him an exasperated shake of my head. He backed off a little, but not much.

"Gresham knows everything," I said. "What could he possibly ask?" Ewan was still throwing off a low rumble, which accelerated at 'knows everything.'

"Actually," Timbra said a bit sharply. "He didn't know you were associating with the Drakontos. He was very surprised to learn I'd met Stryde before at the restaurant…of course, so was I."

"Oh, shit," I said. "I'm sorry, Timbra. He just showed up that day at the restaurant. And I should never have brought him to that party. It was a stupid, stupid call. I felt sorry for him, and I put all your lives in danger. I'm so sorry."

"We're all fine. No one got hurt," Timbra said generously. Of course she couldn't know about Eiven and Stryde.

"What else? Did you tell them everything? About my mom?" I looked to Ewan. "Did you tell them about the other Drakontos?"

"We were honest," Ewan said, "but we didn't offer up any more information than we had to. I think it's safe to operate on the assumption that you don't have any more secrets. You'd better warn the Drakontos there's a search on for them."

"They're gone," I whispered and pulled my knees up. I held my legs to my chest and buried my face in them until the threat of tears passed. "Eiven and Stryde are dead. And Bay left for god knows where in search of my mother."

No one asked how it came to be that Stryde and Eiven had died. Maybe they feared I'd done it. At that moment I didn't feel like reliving the nightmare, and just let it go unsaid.

"What now?" Timbra asked. "What do we do now?"

Ewan's chest expanded on a deep breath. "Now we help Stella hide—and survive—until all this settles down."

Moonlight reflected in the chocolate-colored curls surrounding Ewan Bristol's rugged face. In the months I'd known him he'd always been broody, too clever by half, and so handsome my brain gushed oxytocin simply at the pleasure of looking at him.

But in that moment—when he knew all my secrets, my deficiencies, and the danger my future held—when he threw his fate in with my own... In that moment, I saw Ewan Bristol for the first time.

Thank You for Reading!

Dear Reader.

I hope you enjoyed Book Two in the Descended of Dragons series, *Origin Exposed.* Were you shocked with the way things progressed between Stella and Gresham? Are you Team Gresham or Team Ewan? Readers seem to be about half and half…poor Stella!

Book Three in the series, *Betrayal Foretold*, is set to release late Spring 2016. I think you're going to love it. You won't see some of the twists and turns coming. And don't worry—there's plenty more of both Gresham and Ewan.

Thank you for choosing to read this book. I love feedback; love hearing from readers. Tell me what you liked, what you loved…even what you didn't love. You can write me at authorjencrane@gmail.com or visit my site at www.JenCraneBooks.com

Lastly, please consider leaving a review of *Origin Exposed* wherever you buy books.

Thanks so much for reading, and for supporting me and my books.

Jen

Look for *Betrayal Foretold,* Book 3 in the Descended of Dragons series, in the spring of 2016.

About the Author

jen crane
life's *too real*
for nonfiction

Though she grew up on a working cattle ranch, Jen Crane has been into fantasy and sci-fi since seeing a bootleg tape of *The Princess Bride.*

Jen has a master's degree, and solid work histories in government and non-profit administration. But just in the nick of time she pronounced life *too real* for nonfiction. She now creates endearing characters and alternate realms filled with adventure, magic, and love.

Jen is happily living out her dream in The South with her husband and three children, striking that delicate balance between inspiration and frustration.

Sign up for sneak peeks, news and giveaways at
http://bit.ly/Jen_Crane_Newsletter

www.JenCraneBooks.com
Facebook: JenCraneBooks
Twitter: @JenCraneBooks
Pinterest: JenCraneBooks
Instagram: JenCraneBooks
Tumblr: JenCraneBooks

Made in the USA
Columbia, SC
01 April 2025

56027589R00117